SIX CROWS GOLD

VERNON OICKLE

Cover image: Denis Cunningham
Editor: Andrew Wetmore

ISBN: 978-1-990187-57-5
First edition December 2022

2475 Perotte Road
Annapolis County, NS
B0S 1A0

moosehousepress.com
info@moosehousepress.com

We live and work in Mi'kma'ki, the ancestral and unceded territory of the Mi'kmaw people. This territory is covered by the "Treaties of Peace and Friendship" which Mi'kmaw and Wolastoqiyik (Maliseet) people first signed with the British Crown in 1725. The treaties did not deal with surrender of lands and resources but in fact recognized Mi'kmaq and Wolastoqiyik (Maliseet) title and established the rules for what was to be an ongoing relationship between nations. We are all Treaty people.

Also by Vernon Oickle

One Crow Sorrow
Two Crows Joy
Three Crows a Letter
Four Crows a Boy
Five Crows Silver

Life and Death after Billy
Friends & Neighbours: a collection of stories from the Liverpool Advance
Busted: Nova Scotia's War on Drugs
Queens County
Ghost Stories of the Maritimes (volumes 1 and 2)
Dancing with the Dead
Great Canadian Ghost Stories Volume II (co-author)
Disasters of Atlantic Canada: stories of courage and chaos
Canada's Haunted Coast: true ghost stories of the Maritimes
The Editor's Diary: the first 13 years
Angels Here Among Us
Red Sky at Night
South Shore Facts and Folklore
I'm Movin' On: the life and legacy of Hank Snow
Beaches of Lunenburg-Queens
Nova Scotia Outstanding Outhouse Reader
Red Coat Brigade
Ghost Stories of Nova Scotia
Kiss the Cod!
Strange Nova Scotia
Newfoundland and Labrador Outrageous Outhouse Reader
Where Evil Dwells
How to talk Nova Scotian: the Bluenoser's book of slang
The Nova Scotia Book of Lists
My Nova Scotia Home:
We Love Nova Scotia: a people's portrait
More Ghost Stories of Nova Scotia
Queens County: a history in pictures
The Second Movement: Nova Scotia's outrageous outhouse reader No. 2
So you think you KNOW Nova Scotia?

One crow sorrow, two crows joy;

three crows a letter, four crows a boy;

five crows silver, six crows gold;

seven crows a secret yet to be told;

eight crows for a wish;

nine crows for a kiss;

ten crows for a time of joyous bliss.

**- One version of a common
Nova Scotian folklore verse**

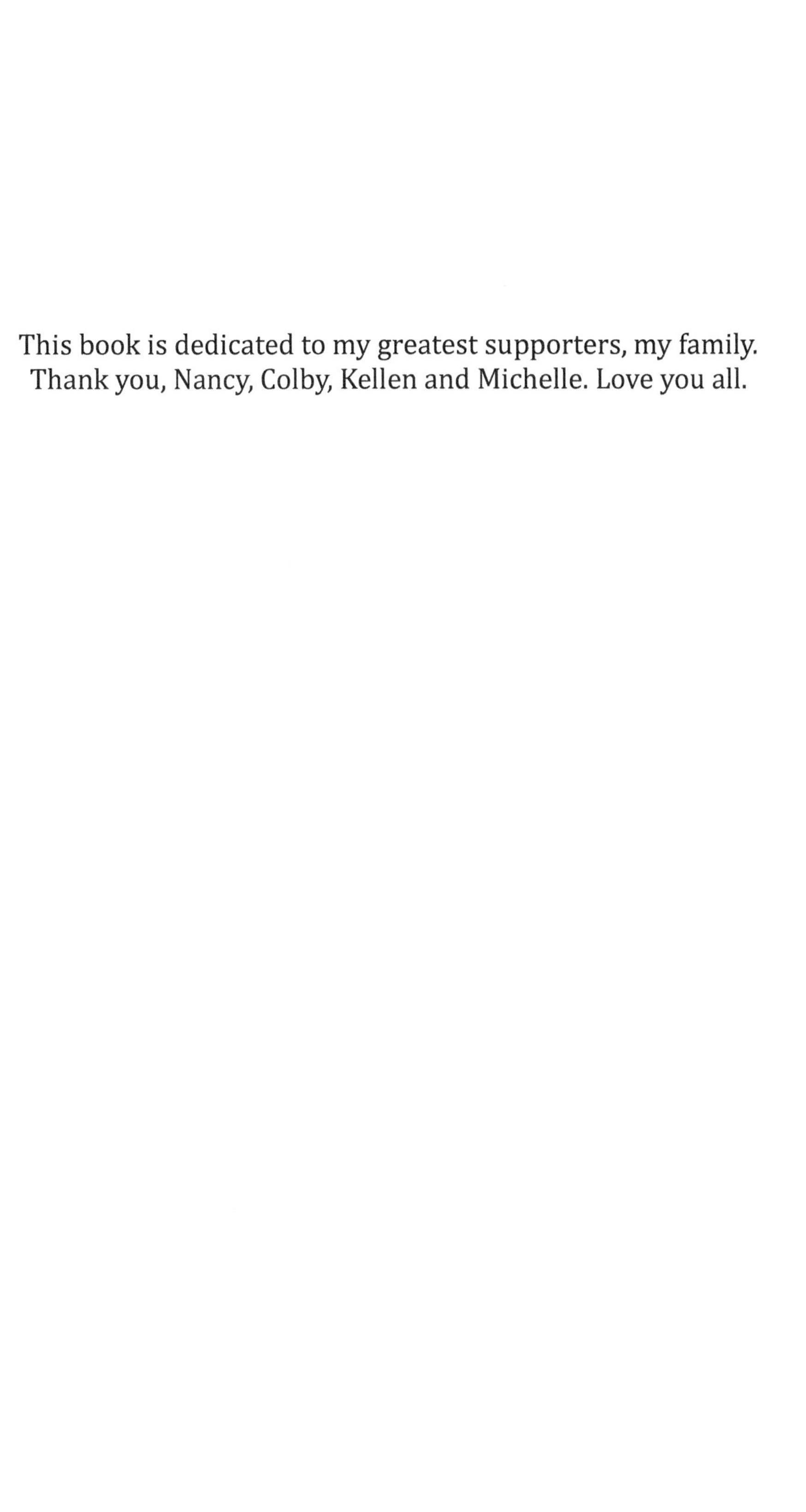
This book is dedicated to my greatest supporters, my family.
Thank you, Nancy, Colby, Kellen and Michelle. Love you all.

This is a work of fiction. The author has created the characters, conversations, interactions, and events; and any resemblance of any character to any real person is coincidental.

Prologue

Their mournful caws fill the night sky. Their anguish, to all who can understand, is palpable.

They are six birds. Chosen to find the powerful force to lead them into the next century.

They call to encourage the supremacy they seek—the keeper who will make their world complete.

They have been without a keeper for two years. And it is the keeper who is their *raison d'être*.

Their last keeper, the woman, was with them for a long time. She gave them purpose, and in the two years since her passing they've been lost, without guidance or direction.

When she died, a part of them died with her. But they know there is another one somewhere. There must be. There always is.

It is their mission to find the one.

But where? Where is she? Or he?

They fly endlessly, patrol upon patrol, perching on rooftops, hiding in the leaves of trees, always listening. Always observing. But nowhere, nowhere can they find their human soulmate. Where is the one who will rise up and take her place?

They sense the time is near. It is the sacred duty of the black six to find the golden one. They will keep looking until their quest is complete. It is their destiny to find and, no matter the cost, to protect the keeper.

Six Crows Gold

Graduation Day

1: When duty calls

Cliff strains to hear his daughter's name called as he sits in the stuffy high school gymnasium. His pride is a beacon on a dark, foggy night. He wipes his forehead with the back of his hand, bursting with joy as his daughter crosses the stage to receive her diploma.

Carly Graham. High school graduate and future marine biologist, he thinks.

She shakes the principal's hand, turns towards the audience and, with a smile as wide as the Mersey River, she waves at him.

How has she grown up so quickly?

Gone is the skinny little girl who used to crawl up on his lap with a book and ask him to read to her. In her place is a confident young woman, her head full of dreams.

His mind flashes back eighteen years. Back to when his then-wife Julie told him she was pregnant, to when his only daughter was born, to when they brought her home from the hospital, to when she took her first step and when he heard her say "Da Da" for the first time.

Leaning forward in the cheap orange plastic chair which has left his ass numb after two hours of sitting on one of the hottest days this year, he fights to keep back tears of pride and joy.

Though it's an odd time to dwell on the past, he remembers the empty years following his divorce, when Julie took his children to Vancouver. Then his mind jumps to when Carly came back to take care of him following his heart attack and surgery. These past three years have been among the happiest of his life. He cherishes the special bond he and his daughter have created.

What will fill the gap when Carly starts Dalhousie University in the fall?

His eyes mist over. But Halifax is less than two hours away, and she can come home every weekend if she wants to.

He chuckles a bit. Knowing Carly, she'll be involved in everything going, and he will most likely have to visit her if he wants to see her. But that's okay, too. This was life.

I am so lucky she is staying in Nova Scotia for university. The full scholarship to Dal had been a blessing.

He jumps as someone grabs his shoulder.

"Cliff?" Julie whispers. "Did you hear what I said?"

"What?" he says, turning to face his ex-wife, who's come to town for the graduation. She'll be returning to Vancouver in two days, following the celebrations.

"Where were you just now?" she asks, smiling.

"Just thinking," he answers, returning her smile.

He and Julie have remained close friends, not only for their children, but because they genuinely like each other. He believes the only reason they separated in the first place was that they were paralyzed with grief over the death of their oldest son, Brian, who was killed by a drunk driver. The accident happened shortly after they moved to Liverpool, when Cliff transferred here with the RCMP.

In time, they found some peace, and moved forward, as much as one could, from that tragic time in their lives.

"It's hard to believe our last child has finished high school," he whispers, thinking about his two other children who are now young adults.

"It sure is," Julie nods. "Carly has grown into a beautiful young woman, Cliff. She's done very well with you here in Liverpool. It was a good move to let her come back to live with you. God knows what would have happened to her if she had stayed out there with me and had to deal with those bullies. I hate to think about it."

"She's pretty special," he agrees.

The audience breaks into applause. Julie says, just loud enough for him to hear, "Cliff, we need to talk before I go back to Vancouver. Just you and me. Can we make some time for that?"

"Sure," he nods, following his daughter with his eyes as she takes her seat back in the section reserved for graduates. "About what?"

"Not now," she replies, raising her voice so he can hear her over the noise as they announce the name of the next graduate. "Later this evening, after Carly and her friends to go to the Safe Grad party. But it's important."

"No worries," he replies.

Then he feels the cell phone vibrate in his pocket. "Shit," he sighs, "I know this won't be good. I left strict orders not to bother me unless it was a matter of life and death."

He scans the text message from dispatch.

"What is it?"

"Not freaking good at all."

Homicide reported, the short message reads.

He turns to Julie. "Give Carly a hug for me and tell her I'll see her later. Tell her I'm very proud of her."

And with that, Cliff stands up and leaves the sweltering building as quickly as he can without causing a disturbance.

Vernon Oickle

Three Days Before

2: Secrets

Secrets.

Everyone has them.

Everyone protects them.

Sometimes going to great lengths to keep them well guarded.

Sometimes even taking them to the grave.

Lily Pittmann rifles through the drawers of the antique oak desk that has been a fixture for decades in the stately Goodwin mansion, the home she shares with her common-law husband, Josh, and their family.

And she hates it.

He keeps things from her. For her own good, he tells her.

"He's keeping me in the dark, and I've had enough," she mutters. "He doesn't trust me. Obviously. I should know everything about him. Everything." She snorts. "And he says he wants me to be his wife!"

Looking for any clues that might tell her what he's up to, she pulls some documents from the back of a drawer and scrutinizes them.

"Nothing," she sighs, raising her hand to rub her eyes.

I want to know exactly what's going on. He can't keep me in the dark like this. I'm going to be caught off guard. I won't be prepared. Oh, what's the point? I've told him this a thousand times and he treats me like I'm a stupid underling. Like I'm not clever enough to share his world.

She slams the second desk drawer shut. *He's being stubborn. So damn stubborn. These secrets are going to destroy our relationship. Maybe even destroy him. Or us!*

She stands up straight and twists her shoulders left to right to shake off the stiffness from bending over the files for so long. For no reason she can fathom, the hairs stand up on the back of her neck.

She looks round the room. She is alone.

"Alone, and maybe going crazy," she whispers. "Now I'm even talking to myself. Good lord. What next?"

She leafs through the stacks of papers and documents stuffed in the desk drawers, continuing her search for clues. "Josh is smart and he isn't likely to leave anything just lying out in the open for the whole world to see."

She half-smiles. "He knows I snoop when he's away so he's likely covered his tracks. Perhaps he was careless this time."

Her eyes narrow. She knew she is obsessing over it, but his secrets had become a storm cloud hanging over their relationship.

And Lily fears a tempest's fury was about to strike. Her feelings of deep anxiety and apprehension are sometimes so intense she can hardly breathe; so powerful they keep her awake at night. And, while she hates to admit it, lately she fears she has been harbouring a sense of loathing toward the man she'd built a life with. She doesn't like having these feelings.

She knows Josh loves her. She is sure of his feelings and she believes she still loves him, but their six-year relationship has been marred by his secrets. Although he has asked her on repeated occasions to marry him, it is those skeletons in the closet that keep her from saying yes. Until he comes clean, she refuses to wear his ring. It's the one trump card she holds in their relationship and she isn't about to relinquish that power just yet.

It's simple, she's told him many times. If he wants to marry her, then he can't hide things from her.

Still, he refuses to divulge anything about his elusive business partners in the United States. He won't tell her who they are or what role they play in his affairs, and lately she feels, it has gotten worse. *It's as if he's a spy engaged in covert affairs for the Canadian government or some secretive police force*, she thinks. *Could it be true?*

Reaching for the bottom drawer on the right-hand side of the desk, she finds it's locked. Wondering where he might hide the key, she continues to tug on the drawer's round, brass handle, but it won't budge.

"Goddamn it."

Her suspicions are confirmed. "He *is* hiding something."

Giving the handle one more futile tug, she briefly contemplates getting the crowbar from the garage and battling this antique locked desk once and for all. She is truly sick and tired of the espionage.

"I'm the mother of his son, we've lived together for six years and we are business partners. We should share everything. If he's done something illegal or immoral, I can forgive him, maybe even help him deal with whatever it is, but oh my fucking god this makes me mad."

"Who are you talking to, Nan?" The boy's voice startles her. She had thought she was alone in the den.

She quickly spins around in the leather swivel chair to face her seven-year-old grandson. He's standing near the desk and studying her every movement. Lily and Josh have been raising the boy ever since his mother, Gwen, abandoned him three years ago and headed out west with some drug addict who had never held a full-time job in his life. She'd only heard from her daughter on rare occasions since she'd gone to Alberta and hadn't seen her in all that time.

In truth, Lily knows very little about her oldest child's existence, other than that she was living in Calgary and supposedly working as a waitress the last time she heard from her, about three months ago. But she was sure Gwen's drug problems had not gotten any better because, if they had, Lily believes her daughter would come home to be with her son. She has no doubt Gwen loves her child, but merely lost her way, falling in with the wrong crowd. She's thankful Gwen left her son behind instead of dragging him off to live in some crack house with addicts and perverts. God knows what would have happened to the little boy then. She shudders at the thought.

"Hello, my darling boy. I was just muttering to myself. How are you doing, Carter?" She smiles at the stocky boy who, even at his age, has developed a reputation around town for being a loner. Other than Hunter Henderson-Webster, the adopted son of Samantha Henderson and Kate Webster, Carter has no friends. For some reason people in town consider Carter odd. Other children pick on him, ridicule him and sometimes even resort to physical bullying.

She knows secrets can eat you up from the inside out, destroy relationships and lead to a world of hurt. It breaks her heart that his personal situation is a mystery to her.

Another one, she thinks, smiling a little at the black humour of it. Carter is a thoughtful, caring, generous and polite little boy. She's raised him to have good manners and she is especially proud of how well he's managed to adapt to his situation despite the attitudes of others.

"I thought you were upstairs playing with Alex."

"I was," Carter answers, his speech very soft, a reflection of his personality and disposition. "But I'm hungry. Can I please have a snack?"

"There are some grapes in the fridge, if you want those." She smiles at him while pushing her long red hair back behind her ears. "It will soon be lunch time so you can't have too much right now or you will ruin your appetite."

"Okay, Nan," he nods and turns to leave the den. "Thanks. I like grapes."

"You're welcome." She takes the boy by his shoulders and turns him to face her. "Is everything all right, Carter?"

"Yes Nan," he nods.

"Come on, Carter." She brushes his tussled black hair back from his forehead. "You know it's no good to lie to me. I can tell when something's bothering you, so tell me what gives."

"Nan," he whispers. "It's nothing."

"Tell me, honey. What's going on?"

All right. I want to play soccer this summer with all the kids from my class, but they say I'm too fat to run." Tears pool in his eyes and slowly roll down his cheeks.

"Who says you're too fat to play?" she asks, her voice soft and soothing.

"Everybody."

"Now, Carter, I can't believe 'everybody' says that. Who exactly is everybody?"

"Some of the kids at school."

"Such as who?"

"Hunter says it."

"I can see why it would upset you." Lily wipes away his tears with her hand. "He's supposed to be your best friend and he shouldn't be saying bad things to you. I'll talk to his moms about it. Maybe he just doesn't understand how hurtful it is. Did you tell him it hurts your feelings when he says such things?"

"No, Nan. I didn't want to make him mad at me."

"If he's your friend, Carter, he shouldn't get mad at you if you're honest with him. Friends don't hurt each other. I think he needs to know his words make you feel bad."

"He won't play with me anymore if you yell at him."

"I'm not going to yell at him. I'm going to speak with his moms and they'll talk to him. I bet Hunter doesn't fully understand what he says can sometimes hurt other people. It will be okay." She smiles at him. "I promise."

"Okay, Nan."

"Anything else?"

"Well, I was wondering when Gramps is coming home?"

"It will be a couple more days, Carter. He's on another business trip."

"Where does he go, Nan?"

"To the States, or so he tells me."

"Okay," he replies. She knows he has no idea where or what 'the States' are.

"Give me a hug and then go and find those grapes. I've got to go check on Alex and then I'll make us some lunch. How about tacos? And since it's a nice day we could eat on the back patio."

"Thanks, Nan."

Watching her grandson leave the room, she wipes the tears from her eyes. *Well, that's a problem that needs a fix right away, and I know just what to do. No one bullies my family and gets away with it.*

Lily heads down the hall to the ornamental staircase that leads to the mansion's second level and climbs the steps, making a mental note to speak with Samantha and Kate about the situation with their son. They are among her best friends in Liverpool and she is sure they would want to address the matter before it escalates. They are very strict with their adopted son and try to teach him the difference between right and wrong.

But she finds her mind dodging away from this straightforward problem, back to her husband and his evasions. *Either he comes clean or it's over, once and for all.*

3: Mysterious trips

He turns the water on as hot as he can stand it, and stands in the shower for what seems like an eternity, almost doubling over as guilt and remorse course through him.

The truth, he's convinced, would kill the woman he loves. It's best if some secrets never see the light of day, of that he's sure. Even if it means deceiving Lily and his family.

"Maybe I should just tell her and let her decide if I deserve forgiveness," he mutters to himself, watching the steaming hot water swirl down the drain. "I hate keeping these things from you, Lily, honey. It's killing me. And I know it's going to kill you, too, unless I tell you the truth."

He groans. "But it's bad. It's so goddamned bad. It's the worst thing one human being could do and keeping it from the one I love makes it even worse. But I'm so afraid that you'll hate me. So afraid you will just up and walk out the door."

He stands in hot water for another ten minutes washing his hair and roughly scrubbing his skin. *Hot water*, he thinks. *Oh yeah. I am definitely in hot water. In so many fucking ways.*

Telling her these excursions are business trips designed to meet anonymous investors who had been part of the Goodwin family empire long before he became involved with her, Josh has been going to New York City for several years now.

He steps out of the shower and dries himself off with the plush white hotel towel. In truth, these trips have nothing to do with the family business.

Nothing, he thinks as he stares into the large mirror above the ivory-coloured vanity. *Absolutely nothing.*

"But I am totally screwed. I can't stop making these trips. And, to be honest with myself, I don't want to. I love the way I feel when I am here. It's ruining my life with Lily, but I need these trips. I *need* them." He sighs. "And I will find a way to make this all work without hurting her. It won't be easy, but I have to."

It took careful planning to pull off these trips and to cover his tracks. He knows Lily is looking for answers and he appreciates her intelligence. He would never underestimate her resolve to finding out the truth.

He chuckles. "She's relentless when she sets her mind to something, so she's not about to give up any time soon. She's so damn sexy when she's like that, and I love that about her. I am a goner. She probably has figured it out already."

But how could she?

His mind skims his *modus operendi*. Whenever he travels to New York he never follows a routine. He travels at different times of the year and he varies the duration of his visit, sometimes staying only two or three days, other times staying a week to ten days. He comes here via different routes, sometimes flying direct from Halifax, but sometimes through Montreal, Toronto or Ottawa. Sometimes even through Boston. And when he is in New York he uses a different fake name each time, and stays at different hotels and never goes to the same restaurant or shops at the same stores more than once on any trip. On top of all these precautions, he pays for everything in cash. Credit cards and debit are strictly forbidden when he's on these trips.

Would Lily follow me? he wonders, combing his hair into place.

He doesn't think she would, but he can't really be sure.

Would she hire someone to track me down?

Perhaps. If she were desperate enough, he believes, but he doesn't think it has gotten to that point just yet.

With almost eight hundred hotels in New York City and thousands of restaurants to choose from, it would be impossible to track his movements unless someone were right on his tail, and he's sure if someone were following him closely, he would have spotted him by now. *I'm not exactly a slouch when it comes to this type of espionage activity.*

His biggest fear in perpetuating these lies was that Lily might actually think he is having an affair with another woman and is coming to New York for a romantic rendezvous, but nothing could be further from the truth. He's tried over and over to assure her of that fact.

Does she buy it?

"To be honest, if the roles were reversed I sure as hell wouldn't believe her. So why would I ever expect her to believe me. Yup. Totally fucked."

He knew in his heart and soul that he never had and never would cheat on Lily. In fact, he'd rather die than hurt her in such a way. He just had to convince her.

Hanging the towel on a hook stuck to the back of the bathroom door, then grabbing his boxer briefs and pulling them on, he hopes he's been able to convince her of his loyalty to her. But deep down, he isn't sure he'd been successful and with each trip he makes he fears the wedge of deceit is widening the rift between them.

Damn it, he thinks, staring into the mirror again. *How did things become so complicated?*

He'd known Lily Pittmann for many years. He first met the fiery redhead with the emerald green eyes at a car dealership, part of his family's empire that his oldest brother, Lance, managed. Despite the fact she was almost ten years older than him, he was attracted to her from the first time they'd met.

He was a bastard, pure and simple, Josh thinks, remembering his brother, who died a brutal death at the hands of a mysterious young woman named Maggie Collins. Collins had blown into town many years ago and decimated his family including his father, Gerald—another bastard—both his brothers, Lance and Max, and an uncle.

The authorities never fully explained the deaths, but the result was that Josh inherited the family's entire fortune and all the business holdings. He'd managed to parley those interests into more wealth than his old man or brothers could have ever imagined.

It was following his family's destruction that he'd gotten to know Lily on a more intimate basis. Reeling from the death of her husband, Tom Pittmann, who had succumbed to the ravages of pancreatic cancer, she was left with raising three children on her own, including Gwen.

"Gwen. The selfish bitch," he mutters, unable to stop himself. Although he loves Gwen's son, Carter, very much and enjoys being a *de facto* father to him, he cannot begin to fathom how Gwen could abdicate her responsibilities as a mother. It really pisses him off. If there is one thing that is important to Josh, it is living up to one's responsibilities when it comes to raising children.

"People who think the world owes them something and go through life with a huge chip on their shoulder are useless. And that's what Gwen is. She's a user. A leach who sucks the life from everyone around her. I hate what she puts you through, baby," he whispers to a non-existent Lily.

He thinks about how quickly he had gravitated to Lily. How he had started to rely on her. With his entire family wiped out, it wasn't long before Josh became dependant on her to run the car dealership while he took care of other business and personal matters. He ultimately made her manager of the dealership and, in time, found himself unable to resist her pull. Eventually, they began dating and, in due course, they ended up living together, but she had never agreed to marry him because... he shakes his head. "Because you don't trust me," he whispers.

Their personal relationship hit new heights almost two and a half years ago when their son Alex was born on Christmas Eve. He was the smallest of twin boys Lily had been carrying, but the second baby, Andrew, died in childbirth of some rare medical complications Josh never did fully understand or accept.

At first, he had a difficult time dealing with the loss of one of his sons, but almost immediately he embraced fatherhood and Alex was the apple of his eye. He was everything Josh could have ever hoped for in a son. The boy was smart and loving, with a great disposition. In fact, Josh sometimes thought the child much more mature than he should be for a two-and-a-half-year-old and he was convinced his son was destined for something great.

Thinking about Alex makes him smile. "And I know every parent believes their child is special, Alex, but I know you are. I can't explain it. I can't understand it. But you are a remarkable human being. There is something…"

He stops whispering to himself for a moment, and thinks about it. *Something powerful in you. A magnetism. I'm not sure what it is, but it is there.*

Josh has not shared his beliefs with Lily. He is afraid she will dismiss his suspicions as nothing more than fatherly pride.

He pulls on his socks and brown Berluti wingtips, which cost him over $1,800, and realizes he is almost late for his reservation. Sliding his black leather wallet into his pocket and slipping on his black Ray-Bans, he glances into the hotel room mirror and admires himself.

Not bad, he thinks.

Deep breath.

He is ready.

As he leaves his fourth-floor hotel room and heads to the elevator, he feels anxious. He's been planning this meeting for several months and he doesn't want to be late.

4: Talking to birds

When Alex was born two and a half years ago, Lily's life changed forever.

At first, she wasn't sure she wanted any more children. By the time she found out she was pregnant with Josh's child, the three children she had with her husband were almost fully grown and she was ready to move on from the demands of raising babies. Since she had put her own dreams on hold when she married Tom, she had determined she was now ready for a new chapter in her life and babies weren't a part of it.

Then, when, she learned she was carrying twins, the news nearly devastated her. She withdrew from everyone and practically gave up living. The emotional stress had become almost too much for her to handle.

But when Alex came into her life on that event-filled Christmas Eve, her outlook changed entirely. She was heartbroken one of the twins, Andrew, was born dead, but she gave herself over to the precious little boy who was born with a full head of black hair, just like his dad.

Now she can't imagine her life without Alex. He is her everything and her entire world revolves around the little boy who has become the embodiment of her dreams, all her hopes and aspirations. She would be lost without him.

Following his birth she stepped back from her busy schedule, putting her real estate business into the hands of a manager. Although she maintained contact with the office, she had removed herself almost entirely from the day-to-day operations so she could spend almost all her time with her son.

Once he started school, she would go back to work full-time, but for now she is content and enjoying her time with him. Hers is almost the perfect world, complete with her son, her grandson, Carter, and a man she loves.

Yes, she thinks, approaching her son's bedroom door, *almost perfect.* Except for the one black cloud that continues to hang over her life, the cloud of secrets Josh insists on keeping from her. If not for Alex, she would have given Josh an ultimatum a long time ago, despite how much she loves him. *Tell me the truth or we're through.*

She can't shake the feeling he is protecting something that might threaten her world.

It would kill Josh if she took Alex and moved out, but Josh was giving her little choice. She can't raise their son in a home filled with distrust and stress, the kind that comes when people have a closet filled with skeletons.

Lily had sensed a long time ago that Alex was special. She'd known it from the first time she held him in the hospital delivery room, but the feeling has grown in intensity over the past two and half years and she is sure Alex has a date with destiny. Although she has no idea what that destiny may be, she is certain that she has to protect and nurture him at all costs, so he can meet it.

Alex walked and talked earlier than any of her other children. He thought and reacted with a maturity level far beyond any other three-year-old she'd ever seen. It was beyond mimicking the actions of others. She had observed him doing things no child his age should be able to do. She'd told no one—not even the boy's father—of what she knew he was capable of doing.

Lily grew up in Liverpool and was aware her family had a history of being connected to some weird and often sensational happenings throughout the centuries in this town, but she'd always dismissed those legends as nothing more than folklore, superstitions and old wives' tales. But now she's not so sure.

She had heard the stories about her great grandmother, Clara Underwood, being a witch, but she never took those things very seriously. She remembers her mother talking about the miraculous things Clara could do. She has vivid memories of visiting the old woman as a child, but as she grew up, she drifted away from her family roots and eventually she had little contact with her great grandmother, although she knows Clara followed her family with a great deal of interest and insisted she be given a photo of each of her children when they were born.

Other than dropping by maybe once a year for the obligatory visit, Lily went out of her way to ignore her great grandmother, fearing maybe someone might think ill thoughts about her because of her family connections and the reputation that came with it.

However, when Clara died two years ago, the old woman left everything in her will to Lily and Alex. It wasn't worth much in terms of money, but she left them the old homestead and property along with all her personal belongings.

Why she would do that, Lily had no idea, as there were other family members out there in the world who may have been more deserving than she. But obviously her great grandmother had had other plans. Lily regretted she had lost contact with the old woman, but after Clara's death there was no way she could reverse what she had done, so she'd learned to accept it.

Lily had come to treasure one of the old woman's prized possessions, the old family Bible, a large black-leather-bound book. In the front, it had pages and pages of entries in various handwriting styles and techniques that went back hundreds of years to one of the town's early settlers.

The entries start with Alexandria Gorham, who showed up in Liverpool around 1760, about a year after the town was officially founded. The entries follow through with births and deaths and other notable family milestones. Lily's date of birth is there, as is her marriage to Tom Pittmann and the birth of their three children. There's the date of Tom's death, and the birth of her grandson, Carter.

The final entry in the old book is the birth of her sons, Andrew and Alex Goodwin. Andrew's date of death is the same as the date he was born.

But the Bible was only one intriguing fact about the family. While at one time she was prone to reject her past, she had now come to respect and embrace its legacy.

Lily had heard local stories, including the legend of Alexandria Gorham. According to the story, the Gorham family was one of the first to settle in these parts and they were important people back then, rich and powerful. But for some reason, Alexandria became an outcast and the early people turned on her and shunned her.

It's not really clear what crime the young woman had supposedly committed—if any—but, according to legend, in the early years most of the locals considered Alexandria almost a saint. They said she could work miracles, and that she did many impressive things to help people when they faced hardships. She was said to have cured sickness, helped to mend animals that had fallen to illness and tended to the destitute when they needed a hand. Eventually, however, others in the settlement came to view her as a witch and turned on her. It appeared that that particular faction had more control over the early settlement than Alexandria's supporters, and they made her an outcast.

Lily recalls hearing that something tragic happened when Alexandria was in her late teens or early twenties, and that many of the settlers chose to blame the young woman because they believed her power was responsible for attracting evil to their village.

Eventually, the townspeople drove her away. Alexandria went into the woods one day and just vanished, never to be heard of again. Shortly after her disappearance, the first reports of unusual crow sightings and behaviour began appearing in the town's history.

According to the information on the pages of the family Bible, Alexandria Gorham had a child, a boy, who was raised in secret by another wealthy family of the time, the Haddons. The boy grew up under their protection and played a major role in the town's early history. Eventually, he found a wife and had several children of his own, some of whom remained prominent in the town's affairs.

Based on the family tree in the Bible, Clara Underwood is a direct descendant of Alexandria Gorham, as are Lily and Alex, of course.

The valuable family heirloom, for whatever reason, is now Lily's.

She feels compelled to protect the book and maintain the family record of events. Her great grandmother had entrusted her with this task and she is going to honour the commitment.

She suddenly realizes Alex had been too quiet for too long.

"Alex, honey," Lily calls, opening the door to a landslide of stuffed animals and a collection of toys designed to stimulate any child's imagination. "What are you doing?"

"Alex?" she repeats, seeing him leaning up against the window glass. "What are you doing?"

"Talking to the birds, mommy," the tiny boy finally replies, his words so soft they're almost a whisper.

"What birds? What are you talking about?"

"Those ones." He points his tiny finger toward the branches of a giant oak tree enshrouding the Goodwin mansion. "Those black ones."

"Let me see." She scoops her son up into her arms and peers out the window. She is surprised to see several large, black crows perched on the branches and staring back at her through the glass. The sunlight bouncing off the birds' sleek ebony feathers turns them an iridescent purple-greenish colour that reminds her of a black onyx ring that belonged to her mother. Somehow her daughter, Gwen, ended up with it after her grandmother died.

"See them, Mommy? Aren't they pretty?"

"Yes, honey. They're very pretty."

"There's six of them, Mommy."

"Six? Are you sure, Alex?"

"Yes Mommy. I counted them."

"Do you see them often?"

"No Mommy. This is the first time. What are they?"

"They're crows, Alex. And sometimes they mean trouble."

Her son turns and looks at her, his gaze an intense burn as he shakes his head. "No, Mommy. They will never harm *me*."

5: Who are those boys?

"Alex! Carter!" Lily calls to the boys, who had wandered ahead of her and are running down the sidewalk. "Don't rush or, just as sure as I'm breathing, one of you will fall and hurt yourself. It will be too late once one of you gets hurt."

With lunch out of the way and the kitchen neat and tidy—she prefers to do her own housework even though Josh wants to hire a housekeeper—Lily decided to take the boys to the park to burn off some of their pent-up energy.

Located on the town's historic waterfront, the park, built on the site of the original Haddon house, is a popular family destination and offers a variety of playground equipment for the boys to enjoy. They have much of the same equipment in their own backyard, but Lily enjoys the interaction with the other parents who take their children there on days such as this one. If there's one thing Lily misses about her job, it is the connection she had with other adults.

She loves her children, but devoting all her time and energy to them makes her feel isolated. When she craves adult conversation, she takes the kids to the park so she can chat with other parents. It's a win-win for everyone involved.

"Okay, guys," she calls as they enter the park's grassy area. She spots Samantha Henderson-Webster sitting on a bench near the riverbank, staring at the harbour water as it laps the rocks lining the shore. Lily decides Sam, whom she's known since high school, will be the perfect company.

"I see Hunter over there on the swings, so you can go and play with him. But, Carter, please keep an eye on Alex. Remember he's a lot younger than you guys and it won't take much for him to get hurt. I'll be sitting right over here on the bench with Hunter's mom where I can see you, so you be careful, okay?"

"Yes, Nan," Carter calls as he races toward the swing set.

"Hey Hunter," he cries. A scrawny, brown haired boy on one of the swings waves back at him. "Let's play in the sandbox."

"Alex, you stay with Carter. If you need me, I'll be right here."

The tiny, black-haired boy nods and then chases after Carter.

"Rough day?" Sam asks as Lily flops on the park bench beside her and sighs heavily.

"Not really."

Lily leans her head back and stares up into the bright blue, cloudless sky just as several crows pass overhead. They startle her for a second, given her recent conversation with Alex, but then she dismisses their appearance as mere coincidence. "Truthfully, the kids have been great. Dare I say it," she chuckles as she turns to face her friend, "they've been like little angels all day. I don't know how I got so lucky."

"Where do I find one of those?" Samantha rolls her eyes, smiling broadly.

"Still having problems with Hunter?" Lily asks, trying to convey her sincere interest in her friend's child-rearing difficulties.

"Some days he's a perfect little gentleman, but other days he can be a little monster. It's like he's two different people—one good and one not so good—and he can change on a dime. I've never seen anything like it....It really worries me."

"I imagine it does," Lily nods, keeping her eyes glued on her children. They have taken up positions in the sandbox. "What does Kate have to say about it?"

"She struggles with it as much as I do, but the doctors say he'll outgrow it," Sam replies, watching as her son jumps from a swing and slowly saunters over to the sandbox, where Carter and Alex have started building a fort. "We've seen so many childhood behavioural specialists since we adopted him I could write a book about the stuff. Sometimes, it really is too much to handle."

"Raising children is a full-time job, that's for sure." Lily sighs again. "The two things you know when it comes to children are that none are perfect and that every child is different. If you count Carter, I've raised five children and they're all different. No two are anything near the same and I guess that's a good thing. They've all got their own personalities, attitudes, tempers and their own way of doing things. I know it's challenging. I've had days when I could just scream and pound the walls, but somehow you have to cope. You'd think it would get easier the older they get, but trust me. It doesn't. It gets different, but never easier." She shakes her head ruefully.

"Thanks for the warning." Sam turns to look at the water. "But there are days even after all these years when I'm still not sure we did the right thing, adopting a child. Kate and I thought we were ready to be parents, but I don't think we were."

"You were," Lily assures her, gently touching her friend's shoulder. "I've seen you guys with Hunter. You're terrific mothers and, I can tell you, when Hunter is at our house with Carter, he is a perfect little gentleman. He's well behaved, uses his manners, and always listens when we speak, so you've done something right. What you have to understand, Sam, is most children test their parents. They push the limits so they can see what kind of boundaries you've put up for them. I think that's what Hunter does with you and Kate. He's smart enough to know if he pushes you far enough he can break you. It's not that he's a bad kid. It's just that he's challenging you."

It's Sam's turn to sigh. "Well, I wish he'd back off for a while. I'm really getting tired and I'm afraid I may be reaching my breaking point."

"You'll get through it, Sam," Lily says, deciding now is not the time to bring up the fact her son has been teasing Carter about his weight issues. Mentioning the bullying right now would only add to her friend's anguish. Even though she is sure Sam would want to know about Hunter, she's not about to make matters worse.

She also knows she has to get to the bottom of Carter's accusations, but this is not the right time to do it, for her friend's sake. "How's business?" she asks instead, deciding to change the subject.

"Busy," Sam quickly answers. "But it's good. I like being busy. I really had no idea when I launched the catering business how much demand there would be for it around here, but I've been pleasantly surprised by how much in demand I've become. I've got a huge graduation party coming up in three days and it's keeping me pretty busy preparing. I've taken a few hours off today to spend with Hunter before I have to throw myself into it full time."

"That's because you're so good at it." Lily smiles at her friend. "You've got a good reputation and your food is fantastic. When you're good at what you do, people recognize it and they want quality so that's why they call."

"Do you miss working? I mean, you were so successful in real estate, I imagine there must be days when you'd like to go to office."

"I'd be lying if I said there weren't days when I didn't miss it. But what I don't miss are the long hours or the rushing around so much. What I really miss, though, is the contact I had with the clients and the people at the office. I'm a people person by nature and I like to interact with others so that's sometimes a challenge for me to be removed from other adults. But don't get me wrong. I have no regrets about stepping back from the business and taking time off. It's been really great having the time to spend with the boys."

"You're lucky you're in a financial situation where you can afford to do."

"I guess I am prying by asking this, but are you and Kate having financial difficulties? Sorry if that comes across as being nosy I'm really not."

"God, no." Sam chuckles. Lily senses a sudden uneasiness.

"I just meant not every mother is able to take a few years off to be with her children," Sam says, "and you're really in an enviable position to be able to stay at home with your boys if you choose to. I know a lot of women who would like to remain at home with their kids but financially they aren't able to do."

"Yes." Lily smiles weakly feeling almost ashamed of her good fortune, but she understands Sam's perspective. After all, it wasn't too many years ago when she was in the exact situation. "I know I am lucky. But it wasn't always this easy for me, either. I didn't have the luxury to stay at home with my other children. I had to work just to make ends meet."

"I didn't mean to imply it was easy for you. I remember when you were in a really bad way, especially when Tom got sick and then right after he died. But, lucky for you, you found Josh."

"Yes." Lily smiles again. She glances toward the boys in the sandbox and notices several other kids approaching. "Lucky for me." Turning to Sam, she asks, "Who are those boys? Do you know them? They appear to be older than Carter and Hunter."

"I think they're some kids from down around the new housing development," Sam replies. "I've seen them here a few times when I brought Hunter to play, but I don't really know them. I'd say they're two or three years older than our boys."

"What do you know about them?" Lily asks, feeling the tension mount. Suddenly, she feels as if she's a tightly coiled cobra ready to spring.

"Not much," Sam shrugs. "Why?"

"Carter's been having some trouble at school with some bullies and I'm wondering if maybe they're some of the kids who are picking on him," Lily answers, keeping her eyes glued to the sandbox, prepared to jump into action at the first sign of trouble.

"I wouldn't know for sure what they're like, Lily, but they do give off the impression as if they own the place. And that they don't appreciate other children in what they clearly think is their territory. You can kind of feel those vibes from them, even all the way over here."

"That's what I'm afraid of….That's exactly what I'm afraid of."

6: In the sandbox

"Can you come to my house to play after we leave the park?"

"I don't know," Hunter answers, concentrating all his efforts on building the sand fort he imagines will be the location for many great battles.

"Come on," Carter pleads, digging into the sand. "Nan just let me get a new game for my PlayStation 4. We can play and you can stay for dinner. I think Nan said we're having barbecue hotdogs and hamburgers."

"Maybe," Hunter replies without looking at the other boy.

"Can you ask your mom?" Carter persists.

"Maybe."

So caught up in their conversation and building their fortresses the boys fail to notice three other children have suddenly moved into the sandbox. They are looking to secure a piece of the real estate, even if it means pushing aside Hunter, Carter and Alex.

"Hey, fatty. Get out of the way."

Carter cringes as he recognizes Dillon's voice. He is one of the kids from school who constantly picks on Carter about his weight and any other thing that seems to catch their interest. It made Carter hate to go to school. He is glad they are out on summer break so he doesn't have to face these bullies every day, and he is disappointed they've somehow found him here at the park.

"What'cha making there, fat boy?"

"We're building a fort," Carter softly answers, choosing not to respond to the taunts.

"Doesn't look like much of a fort to me," Dillon replies. He drops to his knees near where Carter had been diligently working on his sand structure. "You need some help with that?"

He pushes his way closer while the other two boys stand watch over the proceedings as if they are the bully's bodyguards.

"No, I can do it."

"Let me help," Dillon insists. He grabs a handful of sand and slaps it on the turret Carter has been painstakingly building for the past few minutes. "There," he grins as the tower topples over into a heap of sand. "Now that looks better. Stupid fat boy. Can't you do anything right?"

"Hey," Carter protests, his bottom lip quivering. "What'cha do that for? You broke it."

"Aw." He turns to his two snickering companions. "Look: the fat boy's gonna' cry. He's not only fat, he's a mommy's boy, too. Oh, no. Wait a minute." His tone becomes mocking. "You don't got a mommy do you? I forgot. You suck on your grandma's tit. He's a grammy's boy."

"Stop it!" Carter steps back in the sandbox to put some distance between himself and the bigger kid. His face is pale and he feels his entire body tremble. He knows he is no match for this bully and, besides, he hates confrontations.

"Stop it?" Dillon taunts, kicking at the sand and watching it fly at his victim, who is now in the furthest corner next to a smaller boy. "What if I don't? Are you gonna make me stop, fat boy?"

Hunter jumps up. "Just leave him alone, Dillon." He's had enough and isn't afraid to confront the older boy. "Just leave him alone and get out of here. He hasn't don't anything to you."

"You stay out of this, Hunter," Dillon fires back, glaring at the scrawny, brown-haired boy. "This ain't none of your business. It's between me and fat boy here."

"Why do you pick on him?" Hunter asks, raising his face to stare into the older boy's eyes. Hunter would never back down from a fight even if his foe was bigger and older, and even if he thought he might lose, like he knew he would if he fought with Dillon. "What's he ever done to you?"

"Don't push me, Hunter," Dillon sneers, as his buddies crowd around the sandbox, making a shield between the kids and the two women sitting on the park bench near the river. "I ain't talking to you, so mind your own freaking business."

"You're picking on my friend and I don't like it. You're a bully....Just leave him alone."

"I don't wanna'," Dillon fires back. Turning to Carter he adds, "You're so afraid of me, fat boy, that you let your friend fight your battles for you? You're pathetic."

"I'm not afraid of you," Carter says, casting his eyes to the ground. "I just don't want to fight."

"You just don't want to fight," Dillon mocks. "That's 'cause you're a sissy and sissies don't like to fight 'cause they might break a nail. You sound just like my older sister."

"I am not," Carter fires back feeling anger roiling in the pit of his stomach. He hates that his little brother has to witness this abuse.

"You are so a girl," Dillon taunts while at the same time kicking sand at his victim. "Sissy. Sissy, Carter's a sissy. Hey, you know what my pa does? He's just got outta' jail. And he's got tattoos. All over. And he's big and tough. He would tell me to squash a sissy like you."

"Stop!" Carter cries again as Dillon kicks another foot-full of sand at him.

But as he throws his hands up to protect his eyes, the sand suddenly falls back to the ground, as if it had hit an invisible wall.

"What the fuck?" Dillon says. "How'd you do that, fat boy?"

"I didn't do anything," Carter backs farther away, stepping out of the sandbox.

"Yes, you did, you fat creep." Dillon kicks the sand sending a spray toward the chubby kid. "Let's try this again."

Carter throws his hands up to protect his face, and the sand falls again.

"How did you do that, you little fucker?" Dillon screams.

Hunter hurtles forward at that point, ramming his left shoulder into the bully's abdomen, knocking Dillon off balance and sending him backwards. He and the bully tumble to the grass. Dillon lands on his back and Hunter on top of him with his fists flying.

Witnessing the commotion and hearing screams, Lily and Sam spring from the bench. Carter turns and runs toward the two women who are quickly making their way toward the sandbox.

"Nan! These guys won't leave us alone."

"Don't leave Alex there by himself, Carter," Lily calls. "He'll be terrified." She and Sam run towards the brawl.

"Sorry, Nan." Carter turns back to the younger boy. "Come on Alex," he calls. "Come with me."

"No," the small boy answers softly. His body begins to tremble.

"Alex! What are you doing? Come with me before you get hurt!"

In what Carter could only describe as a burst of wind, large amounts of sand fly out of the sandbox and hit the two boys who had been cheering on Dillon. The boys turn and run, deserting their friend.

"Get off me," Dillon shrieks, rolling Hunter onto his back and climbing on his chest. Planting his knees on Hunter's shoulders, he forms his right hand into a fist and raises it back over his head. "You asked for this, Hunter." He swings.

Before the punch lands, however, Dillon feels an invisible force grab him. His arm freezes in place.

"What the fuck?" he screams.

His body suddenly levitates, then flies backward, as if he was a used cleaning rag being flung aside. He hits the ground hard.

Pulling himself up to his hands and knees, Dillon stares at Hunter, who is still sprawled on his back. "How did you do that?" he screams, lurching to his feet. "How?"

Turning to Carter, who is back next to Alex, Dillon screams, "You guys are fucking weird."

He starts to run, to catch up with his two friends, but they have not stopped since they fled from the sandbox. Dillon calls over his shoulder, "This ain't over!"

Hunter rolls over and stands up. "I ain't scared of you or anyone else."

Reaching the sandbox, Lily and Sam quickly fall to their knees to inspect their children.

"What happened? Are you boys okay?" Lily asks. "Who were those guys?"

"Just some boys from school, Nan." Carter refuses to look at her.

"Are they the boys who have been picking on you?"

"I don't know." Carter stares into the distance.

"Don't lie to me, Carter. Are they the bullies?"

"Yes," Hunter answers for his friend. "Yes, they are."

Sam helps her son to his feet. "They pick on Carter all the time," the boy says, as his mother brushes him off.

"Hunter," Sam whispers. "What have I told you about fighting?"

"I know, mom. But they were going to hurt Carter."

"That still doesn't give you the right to fight."

"But, mom—"

"No, Hunter," Lily cuts in. "Your mother is right. You shouldn't fight. And Carter, I don't want you fighting either. You both could get hurt. Those boys are much bigger than you and it appears they are looking for trouble. Fighting never solves anything and someone always ends up getting hurt."

"I wasn't fighting," Carter says.

"One of you must have hit that boy." Lily picks up Alex. "Why else would he run away like that?"

"I don't know, Nan," Carter answers. "I didn't hit him. Honestly, I didn't."

"And I didn't hit him either," Hunter lies, turning to face his mother. He feels his face flush as the words come out of his mouth. "I promise I didn't. I didn't get the chance. I would have, but I didn't have time before he ran away."

He knows he's in trouble, and he can't explain what really happened, and besides, they hadn't seen what happened either. So as long as Carter sticks to the story, he's home free. He crosses his fingers behind his back.

"It's clear we've got a problem on our hands," Sam says to Lily. "The last thing these boys need to worry about is a bunch of bullies."

"Right," Lily sighs heavily and turns to her young son. Alex has remained quiet during the altercation. "Are you okay? Did you get sand in your eyes? Were you afraid?"

"No."

"Okay then, boys," Lily says, glancing at Carter, who has been trying to avoid eye contact with his grandmother. "I think that's enough play time in the park for today. It's time to go home."

"Can Hunter come over and play?" Carter pleads. "We didn't do anything wrong, Nan. Please. Can he?

"That's up to his mom," Lily says. She turns her attention to Sam. "What do you say, mom? Does Hunter want to come over and play for a while? He can stay for supper and you can pick him up later. If it's okay with you, of course."

"What about it, Hunter? Want to go to Carter's house and play for a bit?"

"No, Mom," Hunter shakes his head. He glances at Carter and then the other younger boy. "I don't want to go with them....I want to go home."

"Are you sure? I thought you liked going to play with Carter."

"Yes." He glances again at Alex, and feels very unsettled all of a sudden. What exactly did happen? "I do....But I just want to go home."

"Very well. Sorry, Carter, but I guess Hunter wants to pass for today. Maybe you guys can get together tomorrow."

Carter watches as Hunter and his mother begin to leave the park. Then he turns to Lily. "Why doesn't Hunter want to play with me today, Nan?"

"I don't know, buddy." Lily takes her grandson's hand in one hand and Alex's hand in the other. She holds Alex's hand a little tighter than she is holding Carter's. Despite the heat of the day, Alex's little hand is stone cold.

Suddenly, she feels the hair on the back of her neck rise and a small electrical shock passes through her body.

"Look mommy." Alex points toward a large red maple growing at the edge of the park. "It's the pretty black birds again."

"Yes. I see them, honey. Let's go home."

"There's six of them again," the boy says. "There's six of them, just like outside my bedroom window this morning."

7: No more secrets

It's been a long day, Lily thinks, pulling a pitcher of iced tea from the refrigerator and filling a tall crystal glass. Between the excitement at the park with the boys' run-in with the bullies and her constant worrying about what Josh might be up to, wherever he's gone, she's exhausted. Throw in the suffocating heat and she's just about had enough to deal with for one day.

Iced tea in hand, she makes her way to the back patio, hoping she can enjoy the late-evening sea-salt breeze blowing in from the Atlantic. Maybe she can relax for a bit. Now that the kids are asleep in their beds, she's thinking it's about time she tries to unwind.

Stress makes her feel like she's been pulled through a tiny knothole and then dragged over broken glass. She feels emotionally cut up and bruised. It's been a while since she's felt this overwhelmed but she believes the stress isn't about to go away any time soon, not unless she takes steps to fix what's causing it.

She stretches out on a lime-coloured chaise longue and sits the glass on a table next to the chair. "I've got to get a grip on what's happening in my life," she mutters. "Put everything into perspective. What do I do? I'm going to have a serious melt-down if I can't figure this out. Jesus, I hate Josh sometimes."

She lays her head on the padded cushion and, closing her eyes as the evening sun slowly sinks in the late June sky, focuses on the cool breeze washing over her, caressing her tanned skin. *It isn't fair he's done this to me and the children.*

She sits up quickly. "No more secrets." She reaches for the iced tea just as the phone rings.

"Jesus. Now look what I've done." Startled by the sudden noise she has knocked over her glass and sent it crashing to the patio, where it shattered on the brick. "So much for serenity," she snorts.

She grabs her phone and holds it to her ear. She hates feeling this way. "Hello?"

"Lily? It's Josh. Are you okay, honey?"

"Yes." Her response is quick and curt. "Why?"

"You sound so tired."

"I'm fine."

"You don't sound fine," he continues. "Is everything alright? The kids? Are they okay?"

"They're good."

"What's wrong then?"

"Nothing."

"It's something, Lily," he persists. "I can hear it in your tone. Are you still angry at me for going on my business trip?"

"Truthfully?" She rolls her eyes even though he cannot see her. What did he think? That she is stupid or something? That she could forgive and forget and move on while he keeps his secrets secret? "Pissed, in fact," she replies.

Leaning over, she picks up the shards of glass and puts them in a little pile on the table.

"I thought we discussed this," Josh says. "I thought we had gotten over this impasse."

"We haven't."

"Really?" He seems genuinely surprised. "You're still angry at me for leaving?"

"Yes." She pauses to take a long breath, and then continues, "Yes, Josh. I'm still angry with you and you should know why I'm angry without having to ask. Like I've told you many times, I'm pissed at you for keeping secrets from me. We've got some tough decisions to make when you get back."

"Like what?" She can sense he's worried about what she's implying. "What are you saying, Lily?"

"Not over the phone, Josh," she tells him, sighing deeply. "I don't want to talk about this over the phone."

"You sound like you've made a decision," he says. "You're not going to do anything drastic, are you?"

"Honestly? I don't know what I'm going to do. But I know I can't continue living like this."

"Don't do this, honey," he pleads. "We've already talked about this and you know where I stand."

"I do," she tells him. "And that's the problem, right there in a nutshell."

"I can't do what you're asking me to do Lily. I've told you many times. I just can't break the confidence entrusted to me. Please don't ask me to do that."

"Well then I guess we have nothing else to talk about."

"Honey," he pleads. "Please don't do this again."

"Listen to me. I'm not going to get into details right now, but I want you to think about this while you're away and I want an answer just as soon as you get back. I want you to decide what's more important to you—your secrets or me and the kids."

"Are you giving me an ultimatum?"

"Call it whatever you want, Josh. Just be prepared to tell me where you stand so I know where *I* stand."

"That's not fair."

"I'll tell you what's not fair. It's not fair that you leave here and go god knows where and do god knows what without telling me anything. It's not fair that you've kept secrets from me all these years and you expect me to just sit by without asking questions. It's not fair that you try to manipulate our relationship to suit your purposes. That's what's not fair and I've had enough. I have reached my breaking point."

"Are you leaving me, Lily?" he finally asks. She can sense the emotion in his voice. "I love you very much and I don't know what I would do if you decided to leave me."

"We'll discuss it when you get home, which will be when, by the way? When should I expect you?"

"The day after tomorrow. But please, Lily, try to understand."

"Enough, Josh. No more talk. I've got to go and check on the boys."

"Don't hang up," he pleads. "Let's talk some more."

"No," she snaps. "I'm done talking. Whatever happens next is up to you. My decision rests on your shoulders."

"Come on, honey. We can get through this."

"Goodbye, Josh." She hangs up the phone, wiping her eyes. "Goodbye Josh," she whispers, pressing her head back into the cushion and closing her eyes tightly, wondering if she had been too hateful with him.

She feels herself starting to drift off to sleep when the phone rings again and startles her awake.

"Shit!" She jumps, her eyes snapping open. She feels herself shaking. As she reaches for the phone, she wonders why she's feeling so jumpy all of a sudden. Actually, she thinks, she's been feeling jumpy ever since this morning when Alex pointed out the crows to her.

"Hello," she says into the phone, her words sounding harsh, for she thinks it's Josh calling again.

"Lily?"

She recognizes the woman's voice as Sam.

"Are you okay? Is something wrong? You sound really depressed or angry."

"No, no," she stutters. "Sorry, Sam. It's just…I was almost asleep when the phone rang and it startled me. Sorry about that. I didn't mean to snap at you."

"Don't worry about it. I was just calling to see how the boys were making out. Hunter was a little shaken up after we got back from the park this afternoon and I felt terrible about having to turn down Carter's invitation for him to come by the house to play."

"They're fine, Sam," Lily says. "Actually, they're both in bed and both should be sound asleep by now. So Hunter was having a rough time with the bullies?"

"He was." Sam sighs.

"Who are those kids, anyway, and why are they picking on the boys?"

"I don't know. But if they keep it up, I'll be going to the police about it. Hunter has a tough enough time as it is trying to keep out of trouble. He doesn't need any help from a bunch of hoodlums."

"I know what you mean," Lily says, nodding even though she

knows Sam can't see her. She feels like telling her friend Hunter has also been picking on Carter, but for some reason she cannot find the right words. She sees no need to add to the woman's stress at this point, but she knows she will have to bring it up to Sam sooner or later. "I am really concerned. They seem to target Carter, but I admit I really don't know how to handle this. I know what bullying can do to kids, so I'm afraid if I don't get to the bottom of this, things are only going to get worse for him."

"Maybe we *should* talk to the police," Sam suggests. "Maybe I should call Corporal Graham. He's a good guy and maybe he can help."

"Maybe," Lily agrees, but hesitates. "I'm just afraid the target on Carter will become bigger if the police become involved. I think I have to tread lightly around this for his sake."

"I understand," Sam agrees. "Let's keep our options open, though. And feel free to call me anytime if you need to talk about it."

"Thanks, Sam. I appreciate it." Lily hesitates and then asks, "So what are you guys doing tomorrow? Do you have any plans?"

"Don't think so," Sam says. "I've got a big graduation function coming up in two days so I'm working until about three and then I'm hoping to take a few hours off to spend with Hunter. Kate's taking the morning off to be with him, but then she's going out of town for a few days on some sort of case she's busy with and I'll try to spend as much with Hunter as I can so he doesn't feel neglected. Why do you ask?"

"I was wondering," Lily starts and then stops. "Would you and Hunter like to come over in the afternoon? It's supposed to be another hot day so we can spend a few hours in the pool and then have some dinner. That way the boys can play and we can visit. And we don't have to worry about bullies."

"Sounds great, Lily," Sam says. "I'm sure Hunter would love it."

"Fine, then. Why don't you give me a call when you get off work to let me know when you'll be coming? Carter and Alex will love having Hunter here, and I look forward to the visit."

"Thanks, Lily. I'll be looking forward to it too."

"Bye for now."

Lily puts her phone on the table. She lies back once more, only to be jolted when the phone rings yet again. *Shit. Now who?*

"Hello."

To her surprise, no one answers.

"Hello," she says again and listens for a response.

There is only silence.

"Hello," she says once more as she feels the beating of her heart increase in intensity. "Hello? Is someone there?"

Forcing herself to calm her breathing she listens quietly but still can hear no one on the other end. Suddenly, the phone goes dead and then the dial tone begins.

"Shit," Lily whispers, pressing the talk button to turn the phone off. *That was weird*. She glances around the backyard as the breeze pushes strands of her long red hair up over her head as if they were ribbons.

Placing the phone on the table, she immediately feels cold and alone as the sensations of apprehension she felt earlier in the day wash over her again and grip her, much like an angry adversary would grab their foe by the shoulders and shake them. Rising to her feet, she quietly scans the yard.

The property is awash in a sea of vivid colours from the early summer plants she's lovingly placed and nurtured over the years, her Lady's Mantle, Foxglove, Geranium, Iris, Primrose and Columbine—her personal favourites. She breaths deeply.

She doesn't know for sure why she might think this, but for some reason she believes that call was a warning of sorts, a harbinger that something dark and sinister might be coming their way.

"Shit," she whispers, shivering while the goose bumps race up her spine and gather between her shoulder blades. Six crows have settled softly on the grass not far from the patio.

She didn't see them land, so she has no idea how long they've been there, but she's been around this town long enough to know if crows are visiting her property with such frequency, then something is definitely out of whack.

"What do you want?" she asks the crows, which have been hopping about the yard, ignoring the woman on the patio. "Just go away and leave us alone," she pleads. "I really don't want to deal with you right now."

Hearing the woman's words, the crows stop in their tracks and, on cue, turn to face her.

Suddenly overwhelmed with emotion, she feels the tears begin to fall. "I don't know what you're doing here, but I don't want any trouble," she cries. "Please, please, just leave us alone."

Looking down at her hand, she sees she's cut her finger on the broken glass she'd picked up. She shivers. A rivulet of bright red blood runs through her fingers and drips onto the stone terrace, as Lily starts to tremble.

Something is seriously, seriously wrong.

Two Days Before

8: A calling

"What the hell is going on around here?" Lily mutters and rolls over. She stares at the screen on her phone.

"Jesus," she sighs when she sees it's almost three a.m. She fears that, come morning, she'll be too exhausted to get out of bed. She's always been the kind of person who requires a regular routine of sleep and if she doesn't get at least seven hours of rest each night, she doesn't feel as though she's capable of functioning at full capacity.

But tonight, she fears, blinking again, sleep is eluding her.

"Damn it." She sighs heavily, throws back the thin cotton sheets and slides out of the king-sized bed that seems so empty these days even when Josh is here. *If I can't sleep I may as well do something useful. I may as well review the last quarter reports they sent over from the office….Oh my God. I really live an exciting life. What else could I possibly be doing at three in the morning? And I never seem to have the time to look at them during the day, so why the hell not do it now?*

She slips her feet into the flip flops she'd left at the side of her bed, and stands up. *Reviewing the reports is more productive than laying here tossing and turning with my mind racing, wildly taking me places I'd rather not go right now.* She shakes her head and says aloud, "Dark places. Unhappy places. Angry places. … Fuck this. I'm getting to work."

She slips on a purple cotton robe she'd picked up from the clearance rack at Winners in Bridgewater. It's not that she's cold, as the night was hot and humid, but she likes the feel of the cool fabric against her skin. If the temperatures remain warm like this, it will soon be time to turn on the central air, but that's the least of her worries right now, she thinks. She could live with a little heat and humidity if she could put this feeling of despair behind her.

As if things weren't bad enough, on top of her problems with Josh and Carter's bullies she now has to worry about what the arrival of the six crows means to her and her family. She shudders at the last thought.

"I've lived in this town too long. And I know those damn crows mean something. And that something isn't good," she mutters.

She knows the legends and she's witnessed bizarre events first hand involving the crows. So many in fact, she's worried their appearance can only mean something terrible is about to happen and will involve her or someone in her family.

"One crow sorrow, two crows joy," she whispers as she makes her way from her expansive bedroom, filled with antique furniture, down the dimly-lit hallway to the rooms where the children are sleeping. "Three crows a letter, four crows a boy," she sighs and continues. "Five crows silver, six crows gold…"

She pauses.

"Six crows gold," she says again while wondering about the significance of the number.

"Six," she sighs, reaching Carter's bedroom door and opening it just a crack. *What could that mean? Six what?*

Peering through the opened door and listening at his light breathing, she sees her grandson is sleeping soundly. Content that everything appears to be in order, she eases the door closed again and proceeds to the door of the next room, where her little son is sleeping.

Gold, she thinks, pausing outside the door. *Maybe it's not the number that's important. Maybe it's really gold.*

She takes hold of the door knob, turns it slowly and eases the door open just wide enough so she can peek inside. She does her best to remain quiet, as the last thing she wants to do right now is to wake up either of the children.

Gold? What could that be all about? she wonders. She expects to see Alex sleeping. Instead, she's shocked to find the bed is empty.

"Alex?" She barges into the room and heads directly to the bed.

"Alex," she says again, ripping the covers from the tiny, race-car shaped plastic bed, looking for any clues to the boy's whereabouts.

"Oh my god," she moans. She feels her heart beating faster than anything she's ever felt before. "My sweet boy. Where are you?"

"Nan?"

Hearing the soft voice, she spins around to see her grandson standing in the doorway.

"Carter?" she says. "I didn't mean to wake you. I'm really sorry."

"What's wrong, Nan?"

"Did you see Alex? Is he in your room with you?"

"No. I was sleeping. Is he okay?"

"I don't know," Lily replies. She pushes past her grandson and out into the hallway. "You check the rooms up here and I'll go downstairs to look around. If you find him, call me at once. But be careful, okay?"

"Okay, Nan," the boy says, darting down the hallway.

"Alex," Lily calls, quickly making her way down the winding staircase to the ground level. Her heart is beating so fast she's afraid it may break free of her rib cage. "Alex? Are you down here?"

Reaching the bottom of the stairs, she is in the mansion's grand foyer, with its oak trim and marble floor. She glances around but sees no one.

"Alex?" She pleads as the tears stream down her cheeks. "Please answer me....Where are you?"

She races down the hallway into the kitchen, switches on the light and scans the large room with all its modern appliances. She has everything here she could ever possibly want, but right now all she wants is to find her son.

"Alex," she calls. "Are you in here? If you're playing a game with me I will be very upset with you. I won't be mad, though. I promise. Please tell me where you are."

She's about to head into the large family room when her attention is drawn to the patio.

"Alex?" She gasps, feeling her heart sink to her stomach as she spies her son. He is standing with his back turned to the house and staring off into the backyard so intently it gives her the shivers.

The boy appears oblivious to her presence.

She races to the French doors that open onto the patio, and is surprised to find them unlocked. She always checks them before going to bed and she's positive they were secure.

"Alex, honey?" she calls to him. "Are you okay?" She takes him by the shoulders and turns her son to face her. "What's wrong?"

She pulls him close to her and hugs him tightly. "What's wrong, honey? I was so worried about you. Why did you leave the house?"

"Mommy?" he whispers. "Did you see them?"

"See who, honey?"

"The black birds."

He turns his head to face her and she can see he's blinking wildly as if he's trying to block out a bright light. "Did you see the black birds?"

"Were they here again, honey?"

"Yes."

"Why did you come out here without me? What if you had fallen into the pool?"

"They told me to come out."

"The birds?"

He nods. "Are you angry with me?"

"No, no," she says, trying to look into his dark eyes. "I'm not angry. Just upset you came out here on the patio when I wasn't around. You might have been hurt."

"They told me it would be all right to come out here," he whispers. "They said you wouldn't be angry with me."

"I'm *not* angry, Alex. I was just worried something had happened to you."

"Why are you shaking, Mommy? Are you cold?"

"No, honey. Mommy's fine." She pauses and then asks, "Alex, how did you get out here? The patio doors were locked."

"No, Mommy," he tells her. "The doors were open."

"Are you sure?"

"Yes."

She studies his face. "Did you close them after you came outside?"

"No."

"What did the black birds want, honey?"

"They wanted to tell me something."

"What? What did the birds want to tell you?"

"They told me not to be scared."

She studies his face again and then asks, "Scared of what?"

"I don't know," he quickly answers.

"They didn't tell you?"

"No, Mommy."

"But you heard the birds talking to you?"

"Kind of," he nods.

"What do you mean, kind of?"

"I just heard them. It was just in my head."

She notices his rapid blinking has stopped. "You heard the birds talking to you in your head?"

He nods. A tear trickles from each eye and runs down his cheeks.

"Don't cry, baby," Lily says and pulls the boy close again. Hugging him tightly, she whispers, "I don't know what's going on, but everything will be fine. You don't have to be scared."

"I'm not," he whispers. His voice is soft and gentle. "They told me to never be scared. No matter what happens. To be brave. And fierce like the others. They said I will be fine, Mommy."

She shudders even though she doesn't know why. "What others? Who?"

"I don't know."

"Nan?"

It's Carter.

"He's okay, Carter," Lily answers, smiling at her grandson. "Go back inside. Just give us a minute and we'll be right in."

9: On a ledge

"How dare she speak to me like that?" Josh Goodwin slams his clenched fist against the desk.

"I'm a self-made man. And fucking proud of it. No one gives me ultimatums. No one. Not even Lily, no matter how much I love her. She can't get away with that."

He rolls his bottom lip down, frowning as he continues to fume. There is no one there to hear him, but he has to vent.

"I may have been born into a wealthy family, but they screwed me over six times from Sunday, the bastards. I've earned every fucking thing I own, and I earned it the hard way. Through hard work, blood, sweat and tears. My own. I'm in control of what I do, and who I tell what to. Me. Me. No one else."

He gulps down his poached eggs, already cold and congealing with grease.

"Fucking room service. For what I'm paying they should get this to me while it's still hot."

He slathers butter on his cold toast and eats quickly, washing it down with coffee. "At least that's still hot."

He clicks his iPad open to the morning newspaper and scans the business section, still burning with anger that Lily would have the audacity to put him on notice as she did last night.

"I love that woman, but I won't bow to her pressure."

He skims the lead story on investments and delves into the recent drop in the markets. "What else can go wrong this morning?" he mutters. "If the economy goes to shit, I will lose a fortune."

He decides to send his broker an e-mail to arrange a meeting just as soon as he finishes the paper and his breakfast. He'll try to make a meeting happen as quickly as possible after he returns home tomorrow, but first, he thinks, he's got a lot of personal business to take care of before he can concentrate on other issues.

"Thank God that I have competent and trustworthy people working for me or I'd never be able to stay on top of things." He sighs. "I've got to calm down. Think logically."

Sipping his coffee as he reads the article, Josh contemplates what all of this may mean to his businesses.

"It's looking pretty grim," he mutters. He may have to pull back some of his investments.

His eyes narrow. "I can weather this economic storm, but it may mean making some significant changes, including dumping some of my international holdings. Yes, that's what I can do. It's going to be tight, but I think we can survive."

He sighs heavily, regretting that he may have to take such drastic action. "Fuck. The last thing I need right now is to be distracted by personal problems. Lily is blowing all of this way out of proportion."

He understands she's angry with him for not telling her where he goes or what he does on those business trips. When he promised Lily he was being faithful and wasn't engaging in anything illegal or immoral, he hoped she would trust him. He hoped she would accept his word, but she refuses to let it go.

He cringes as he thinks about the ordeal he faces when he gets home. He knows Lily can be pigheaded and persistent, so he knows he hasn't heard the last of this.

He frowns. *Perhaps I have to just accept the inevitable*, he thinks. *Perhaps everything I wanted for us is about to go up in smoke. Perhaps it is over. One thing I know for certain: if she thinks she can give me an ultimatum without having to deal with the fallout, then she'll always think she can manipulate me. I may as well let her cut my balls off right now.*

Perhaps, he thinks, his concentration veering from the newspaper article, *I should finally call her bluff. Maybe that would settle this once and for all. It's time for us to either move on or end it. She means the world to me, but I'm getting pretty tired of this.*

Maybe, he thinks, taking another sip of coffee, *that's exactly what I should do.*

Whatever he does, though, he's sure he has to put an end to this constant haranguing, for his sake and for Lily's, to say nothing about what all this bickering and backbiting must be doing to the children.

"It's got to stop," Josh sighs.

A sudden and loud 'thud' that sounds like someone throwing a large beanbag against the glass, interrupts his thoughts.

"What the hell?"

He jumps up, spilling his coffee, and runs to the window to peer outside. The morning sky hangs over the city like a large blue cloak. *Surprisingly*, he thinks, *I haven't encountered any major smog problems during this visit. That's a change from other times.*

He notices a thin red smudge on the window about the size of the end of his thumb that he recognizes as the unmistakable smear of blood.

"Jesus," he whispers, pressing his face against the cool glass and scanning the surroundings for any clue as to what may have caused the bloody stains. He fears he already knows the answer.

He sighs deeply, glancing down to a narrow ledge that runs under the fourth-floor window and along the entire width of the building. There, just below the window, he spots a common, brown house sparrow lying on its back with its legs reaching for the sky, continuing to twitch as its tiny nervous system reacts to the sudden shock. It's clear to him the bird has broken its neck from the impact with the thick glass and is now dying.

"Shit," he says, feeling his breath catch in his throat.

"Shit," he says again, backing away from the window.

He knows many people in his hometown consider such phenomena as just natural events with no greater meaning. They discount talk of signs and wonders as nothing more than old wives' tales, born of centuries of superstitions passed down from one generation to the next. But Josh can't help feeling overwhelmed by the presence of the dying bird outside his hotel room.

Recalling the many occasions from his childhood when his mother would talk about such things, Josh remembers her saying that whenever a bird hits a window and dies, it's a sign of impending death. According to the legend, someone close to the family will die within three days.

The room begins to spin. Josh suddenly feels weak and nauseated. With his head violently pounding like someone is smashing it against a wall, he makes his way to the edge of the bed, sits and drops his head between his knees.

"God damn it." He grasps, his head in his hands.

This is the last thing I need this morning, he thinks, as he flops backwards on the bed and closes his eyes. "Shit. Shit. Shit."

Images of his long-dead mother flood back, filling his brain. He hears her words echoing in his ears: "It's true Josh. You'd better be careful. I'm serious. When a bird hits a window, someone you know is going to die. You mark my word."

He hears his mother's voice as clearly as if she were standing right beside the bed, her deep voice, made raspy from years of smoking, making the dire warning seem all the more ominous.

"Get out," he growls. She'd been dead for many years, the supposed victim of a self-inflicted gunshot wound to the chest. He was still young when she died, but he remembers it with such great detail it's almost as if the events happened yesterday.

"Get out of my head, you crazy woman," he screams. His eyes spring open and he stares up at the popcorn ceiling, the white paint turning yellow from years of neglect and the rust-colour water stains confirming it's been a while since the surface saw a fresh coat of paint.

It's not that he stays in dumps when he comes on these trips, because by most standards this is still a nice accommodation. He could afford the finest hotels New York has to offer, but he chooses to stay in less-grand style so as not to attract attention. He's also more difficult to trace that way. After all, he never knows who may be following him, especially now that Lily is so suspicious of everything he does.

He hasn't thought of his mother in many years. He has no desire to remember her now. In fact, he would rather not admit she ever existed because thoughts of her evoke such horrific memories from his childhood that he finds it difficult to cope.

"Not today," he says to no one, pushing himself up into a sitting position and glancing toward the blood-streaked window. He wonders if the tiny bird had finally succumbed to its injuries.

"Not today."

10: Is anyone there?

Placing the boys' breakfasts in front of them on the wooden kitchen table, Lily exhales forcefully and sits in the chair next to her son and directly across from her grandson.

"Alex," she says, smiling at the small boy with the shock of jet-black hair and dark, dreamy eyes. "I want you to eat all your toast and yogurt and drink all your milk. Then you can go outside to play in the backyard."

"Yes, Mommy," he nods and his smile melts her heart. *For someone so tiny*, she thinks, *he packs a lot of punch in one little facial expression.*

"I'm going to sit here with you guys and drink my tea. That way the three of us can chat. Carter, honey, you can go outside after you eat as well, but first I want to talk to you about what happened with those boys yesterday at the park."

"No, Nan. I don't want to."

"I'm sorry, Carter. But this is too serious. When somebody's bullying you like that kid was, it's important that you know you can talk to me or your grandfather or some other adult you can trust."

"But, Nan," he protests between chews.

"No, Carter." She raises her right hand in a gentle gesture, telling him to stop fighting it. She knows they have to discuss this situation, no matter what the boy thinks. She knows when it comes to bullying, it's important to intercede as quickly as possible before the situation escalates. "I want you to tell me everything that's been going on with you and those other guys. You can't keep this bottled up. You have to let me help you."

"They'll get mad at me if I tell you." He swallows his toast and takes a large sip of milk.

"I'll get mad at you if you don't tell me."

She gives him a look that speaks volumes and one her own children have come to recognize. It was futile to argue with her. "Now, come on, Carter. No more stalling."

"Okay." He sighs, and she can see tears welling up in his eyes.

"Honey," she says, taking a softer tone. "I know this is difficult for you, but I can't help you make this stop if you don't tell me what's going on. I promise, once I know what's happening with these bullies, I'll make them stop picking on you. So, tell me. How long has this been going on?"

"Since school started," he whispers, casting his eyes toward the table.

"You mean these kids have been giving you a hard time since after Christmas and you kept it to yourself all this while?"

"No, Nan." He shakes his head. "Since school started after the summer."

"What?" She's stunned. "You mean this has been going on for the whole school year?"

He nods.

"Carter. Why on earth would you keep this to yourself all this while?" she asks as he begins to cry. "I'm sorry," she says. "I am not mad at you. I am, however, upset you didn't come to me sooner. I thought you knew you could trust me."

He says nothing but wipes his eyes with both his hands.

"Okay, now," Lily continues. "Try to stop the tears."

She waits for him to compose himself and then asks, "Why did they start picking on you?"

"They made fun of me because I'm fat," he answers between snuffs.

"You're not fat, Carter." She reaches across the table and takes her grandson's hand. "You're a little stocky. But even if you *were* fat, it still doesn't give them the right to bully you. No one has the right to make anyone else feel bad. So tell me what they've been doing."

"They call me all kinds of names and laugh at me."

"That's not acceptable." Lily shakes her head. "Do they hit you?

Do they have physical contact with you?"

"I don't know," he shrugs.

"Yes you do." She squeezes his hand. "Do they hit you, honey? Tell me, please. I need to know everything."

"Sometimes," he finally says, casting eyes to the tiled floor. She can sense his feeling of helplessness and defeat.

"How?"

"They push me and sometimes they kick me. And once, Dillon punched me in the back."

"Have you told anyone about this?"

"No."

"Not even your teacher?"

"No, Nan." He shrugs again.

"Why?"

"Because they would find out and get mad at me because I told on them. Then they'd only want to hit me some more for being a tattletale."

"You're not being a tattletale, Carter, if you come to someone looking for help because a bully is hurting you."

He continues to stare at the floor.

"Look at me, please."

He raises his face and she can see the tears starting to flow again.

"I want you to listen to me, honey," she says, squeezing his hand again. "I want you to understand. You have done absolutely nothing wrong and you, in no way, are in any kind of trouble because of this. I will take it from here."

"Are you going to yell at them, Nan?"

"No, honey." She smiles at him. "I'm not going to yell at them, but I am going to talk to some people about it. I promise you these bullies won't be bothering you again."

Carter buries his face in his hands. Lily looks away as the boy sobs, deep, hiccuping sounds that tear at her heart.

When he quiets down, she whispers, "Now, no more tears, okay? I want you to finish your breakfast and then you can go outside. I've got some work to do this morning, but it won't take me long.

And this afternoon, we're having company."

"Who?" he asks, looking up at her, his eyes still bright with tears.

"Hunter and his mom are coming over for a swim after lunch, and then they're staying for dinner. Is that a good idea?"

"I guess so."

"Is something wrong? I thought you liked playing with Hunter."

"I do," he replies.

"Are you thinking he'll pick on you again?"

He nods, his eyes downcast. They sit in silence for a bit.

"Nan?" Carter's voice is barely a whisper. "I have something very bad to tell you."

Lily looks at her grandson, almost certain now as to what he is going to say. "What is it, Carter?"

"You are going to be really mad at me."

"I promise I won't be," she whispers.

Carter looks up. His eyes are filled with tears. "I know it's bad to lie, Nan. But I lied about Hunter. He didn't call me 'Fatty.'"

Lily thinks for a few moments. Carter has been through enough. She won't punish him for lying to her. "Is there a reason you told me it was Hunter?"

"Because if I told you who it really was, I knew those other boys would kill me. Dillon said his father just got out of jail. He kills people, I'm pretty sure. He's mean. I'm really scared, Nan. I am really scared Dillon and his father will kill me if I said it was Dillon."

Lily feels a chill run down her spine. *The poor little boy. How he must have been suffering this past year.* "Don't worry about that honey," she says. "I will make sure neither Dillon nor his father ever hurts you. You don't have to be afraid anymore."

"You promise, Nan?"

"I do, sweetheart. I promise."

Carter nods, and a small smile crosses his face. "Thanks, Nan. I've been so scared I'm going to die soon. So scared of those bullies."

He gulps down his milk. "May I be excused now please?"

"You may as soon as Alex finishes his breakfast, too."

She turns to face her son, who has been making steady progress on his breakfast. "I want to talk to you too, Alex, for a minute."

The small-featured boy glances at her but says nothing.

"I want to know whatever possessed you to open those patio doors and go outside all by yourself in the middle of the night," she begins. "You could have gotten hurt."

"The doors were open."

"I don't know how they could be. The last thing I did before I went to bed was to check all the doors and I can promise you those patio doors were locked."

He shrugs.

"What were you doing out there, honey?"

"Like I told you. Looking at the black birds," he whispers gravely.

"Yes, you told me that last night. Are you sure that's all there was? Did you see anybody around the backyard?"

He shakes his head.

"So you just went outside and watched the black birds?"

He nods slowly.

"Who said you could go outside, honey?"

"They did."

"The black birds told you?"

He nods and Lily sighs heavily. She suddenly feels very uneasy again, an oppressive weight resting on her chest. She decides to leave it alone for now.

"Okay, Alex," she says, rising from the chair. "You finish up and I'll start the dishes, but I don't want you to ever do that again. Do you understand?"

He remains unresponsive.

Lily faces him and speaks slowly and clearly. "I don't want you to ever do that again. Do you understand what I'm saying?"

He nods, slowly.

"Good," she says, bending to kiss him on the top of the head. Then she heads toward the kitchen counters.

As she thinks about how to best handle this bullying situation with Carter and worries about what really happened with Alex last night, the ringing phone startles her.

"Jesus."

She quickly grabs her iPhone from the counter next to the sink, says, "Hello?" and waits for someone to reply.

"Hello?" She finally says again after several seconds. "Is anyone there?"

Recalling a similar call last night, Lily quickly glances around the kitchen.

"Carter," she says to her grandson. "Please take Alex and go outside. Stay near the house and keep a close watch on him. I'll be right out."

Watching as the boys push their chairs away from the table, Lily puts the phone to her ear and says, her voice hushed and low so the boys can't hear, "Who is this?"

There's nothing but dead air.

"Why are you calling here?"

There's still no reply.

"Listen," she says as the boys move on to the back patio, "I don't know who you are or what you want, but please do not phone back here again. Do you hear me? Don't call again."

She listens as the phone goes dead.

"Shit," she sighs, suddenly feeling as though a large, icy hand had taken grip of her throat and she's struggling to breath.

"What the hell is going on around here?" she mutters, placing the phone back on the counter.

She's about to make her way to the patio doors when the phone rings again. She snatches it up and says, "I thought I told you not to call again."

"Lily?" She recognizes Sam's voice. "Are you okay?"

"No," Lily slowly answers, fighting hard to hold back the tears. "No, I'm not."

11: Not afraid of you

Carter and Alex glance at each in silence, their eyes wide with fear. And something else—understanding.

They understand one another. From that understanding has grown an instinct to protect the other, and the bond between them runs deep, even though neither boy fully comprehends how it has evolved or how it works.

Alex bends down and grabs a ball. "Let's play," he finally yells.

And on this bright and warm sunny June morning, as the boys kick the soccer ball around the sprawling backyard, they forget everything else. All they care about is having fun and chasing the ball around the well-groomed grass. If there's one part of the yard Josh takes pride in, it's the grass and he hires the best grounds-keeper in town to make sure it's always perfect, cut the perfect length and fully weeded.

"Kick it to me, Carter," Alex urges. "Kick it to me," he says again, laughing as he runs backwards to put distance between them.

"You won't be able to stop it," Carter tells him. He thinks his companion looks tiny compared to some of the bigger kids he's seen playing soccer. "You can't stop the balls when I kick them," he brags. "I'm too big and strong."

"Yes I can," Alex assures him. "I can stop anything."

"No you can't."

Carter hauls his right leg back, then brings it forward and cheers with pride as his foot connects with the ball, sending it soaring through the air and way over the smaller boy's head. "See? I told you you couldn't stop it."

"I can," the small boy insists, glancing skyward as the black and white orb is just about to soar over his head.

Suddenly it stops, as if it hit an invisible wall, and then quickly plunges to the ground in front of Alex, coming to rest at the boy's feet.

"See," he giggles. "I told you I could stop it."

"How did you do that?" Carter asks, rushing up to him and looking at the boy in amazement. "How did you reach it?"

"Don't know," the small one shrugs. "My turn," he quickly adds, grabbing the soccer ball and placing it in front of him on the grass. "You go over there," he says, pointing toward a large stand of birch and oak trees that line the backyard and buffer the property from the nearby street that leads into the centre of town. "Let me kick it to you."

"You can't kick it that far, Alex. It will never reach way over there."

"Yes I can. Keep going," Alex yells as Carter eventually reaches the edge of the trees.

"Okay, then," Carter calls back. "Go ahead and kick it. Let's see how good you are."

"Here it comes."

Alex backs off the ball and then charges forward to smack the ball with the inner side of his left foot.

He watches as the black and white orb lifts from the grass, soars through the air, picks up momentum and keeps going until it glides well over Carter's head and into the woods.

"Alex," Carter calls to the younger boy who is now rushing across the backyard to meet him. "How did you do that?"

"Don't know. I just kicked it."

"Not even Gramps could kick it that far. Now you've lost it."

They both enter the stand of trees and begin searching for the ball through the underbrush and patches of bushes Josh Goodwin has left standing as a buffer between his property and the nearby street. When the Goodwin mansion was built two centuries ago, the nearby street didn't exist. The town built it about ten years ago despite the family's efforts to halt the development.

Based on conversations he has heard at the house over the years, Carter knows all about this land. He knows his grandfather couldn't stop the road from being put through. It was town-owned property and council determined a road in this location would open up land for new development. New houses have sprung up on land that had previously been vacant. And despite his efforts to block construction, Josh actually owned property in the development area, which he promptly sold to a contractor for a huge profit.

"If you can't beat them, take their money," Carter had overheard his grandfather tell his grandmother when he sold the property. "Business is business."

Picking up on Carter's comment about his father, Alex insists, "Daddy could kick it a lot further. He could kick it to the moon if he wanted to."

"No he couldn't," Carter insists. "He's not that powerful. But you fooled me, Alex, with that kick. It was a long ways. Did you see the ball travel? Man, it had some kind of height on it."

"Yes," Alex answers, pushing through the underbrush and following the older boy's lead.

"Be careful not to fall," Carter says. "It's pretty thick in here. Nan would be mad at us if you got hurt."

Glancing around the bushes he asks, "Do you see it anywhere? I know the ball went in right around here somewhere. It's got to be around here."

"I see it," Alex whispers to Carter. "But the other boy's got it."

"What other boy?" Carter asks. He glances where his brother is pointing. "Oh, *that* other boy."

"Are you looking for this, Fat Boy?" Dillon glares at Carter while holding the soccer ball. He is standing next to a large birch tree.

"What are you doing here?" Carter's hate for the boy who has been bullying him comes through loud and clear in his words.

"Just hanging around," Dillon taunts. "Not that it's any of your business."

"Just leave, Dillon, okay?"

"Why? I'm just standing here. Besides, you don't own these woods. You can't tell me what to do."

"Yes we do," Carter fires back. "Gramps owns all this property, so just get out of here and leave us alone."

"I don't think so, Fat Boy." Dillon tosses the soccer ball into the air and then catches it again. "I think I'll play some soccer." Tossing the ball into the air again, he adds, "I just found this nice ball laying right here on the ground. It's a good one."

"Give me my ball," Carter demands.

"You want it, come and get it."

The two boys who were with Dillon yesterday at the park suddenly emerge from behind a thick clump of bushes.

"Come and take it, Fat Boy."

"Come on Dillon," Carter says, keeping his distance from the trio of older and bigger boys. "Just give me the ball."

"Why should I?"

"'Cause it's mine."

"Who says it's yours?"

"See there? It's got my initials on it. CP. Carter Pittmann."

"That's not you," Dillon laughs. "Your initials are FB for Fat Boy."

"I'm not fat."

"'I'm not fat'," Dillon mocks. "'I'm not fat'."

"No, I'm not."

"Come on Carter," Alex says, pulling on his brother's arm. "Let's go back to the yard. We can get another ball."

"No." Carter pulls away. "I want *my* ball."

"You should listen to your little brother, Fat Boy," the bully tells him. "This is my ball and I think I'll take it home with me."

"Just give me my ball, Dillon, and then leave," Carter insists. Cocking his head in the direction of the bigger boy, he adds, "I'm not afraid of you."

"If you think you can make us leave, go right ahead and try," Dillon says. "Come and take this ball if you want it."

"Come with me, Carter," Alex says. "Let's go or I'm going to get Mommy."

"No way," Carter says, inching closer to Dillon and his two companions. "I'm not going anywhere until I get my ball back."

"Well I'm not giving it to you." Dillon turns the ball in his hands. "I like this ball. I can tell it's one of those expensive ones. I think I'll keep it."

Deciding he's had enough, Carter charges the older boy and tries to grab him by the arms. "Give me my ball, I said. Give it to me right now and get out of here."

"Are you fucking stupid, Fat Boy?" Dillon tosses the ball to one of his cohorts. "You're not getting the fucking ball."

He pushes back, causing Carter to stumble backwards and trip over a branch close to the ground.

"Ow," he cries out as he falls on his back with a thud, striking his right elbow on a nearby rock. Despite his most valiant efforts to hold back the tears, he can feel them trickle down his cheeks.

"Crybaby," Dillon sneers. His companions break out into laughter.

One of them throws the ball back to Dillon, and he raises it high over his head like he's getting ready to throw it at the boy who is sprawled on the ground.

"Give him the ball," a harsh, raspy voice cuts through the bushes.

Thinking it's an adult, Dillon drops the ball and spins around.

"What the hell?" All he sees is young Alex staring blankly at him. "You're telling me what to do, little boy?"

"Give him the ball," Alex commands, his voice deep and emotionless.

"Stay out of this kid," Dillon replies. "I got no problem with you. This is between me and your fat brother."

"I said to give him the ball," Alex repeats as his brother slowly pulls himself up off the ground.

"Listen to him, Alex," Carter whispers. "Or he might hurt you too."

"Yeah, you better listen to me, kid," Dillon says. "Keep your nose out of stuff that ain't none of your business. Just go back to your mommy."

Alex glares at the bully. Finally, between clenched teeth, he says, "Give him the ball. Now."

"You mean this ball?" Dillon asks as he retrieves the ball from the ground. "This one?" He hauls back his right arm. "If he wants it so bad, he can have it." He throws the ball directly at Carter's head.

Carter ducks, raises his hands to protect himself, and then watches in amazement as the ball suddenly stops, as if controlled by some sort of unseen force. Then, as if compelled by an invisible hand, it flies back toward Dillon, moving with such speed it's impossible for anyone to react.

Carter watches the ball strike Dillon's face. The sound of ball on skin is loud.

"Fuck!" Dillon claps his hands over his face. "What the fuck?" Globs of blood rush from his nose.

"My nose," he cries, falling to his knees.

His two followers back away from the mayhem, then turn and dart from the woods.

"What just happened?" Carter says to Alex.

The small boy only shrugs.

"How did you do that, you fucking freak?" Dillon cries, wiping the blood from his face and struggling to regain his footing. "How did you make the ball turn around like that?"

"I didn't do it," Carter quickly answers. "I didn't touch the ball."

"Yes, you did," Dillon insists, putting distance between himself and the other boys. "Yes, you did. You had to."

"I didn't," Carter insists.

The older boy turns and runs from the woods.

"I didn't," he calls, but all he hears is Dillon's scream as he runs away.

To Alex, Carter asks, "Did you do that?"

"No."

"Are you sure you didn't do that?"

Alex stares blankly at his brother and shakes his head. "No, Carter. I didn't touch the ball."

"Come on, then," Carter says. He picks up his soccer ball and grabs the small boy by the hand. "Let's get out of here before they come back."

Looking at the red smudge on the ball, he adds, "I need to go back to the house and clean off my ball."

"They won't come back," Alex whispers.

"You never know with those guys," Carter replies. "And I'm not waiting around to see."

"Why do they call you names, Carter?" Alex asks as the two boys make their way from the stand of trees.

"I don't know."

"Why do they hit you?"

"I don't know," Carter sighs, huffing loudly as they head across the backyard toward the house, where they know Lily has been finishing up her work. "They just do."

"Why?"

"I guess they don't like me," Carter admits.

"Why don't they like you?"

"Why do you ask so many questions?" Carter says. "I don't know why they don't like me. They just don't. Okay? Now, do me a favour. Please don't tell Nan what happened."

"Why?"

"Because she'll be mad that we went into the woods and we were fighting and she'll want me to talk about it again. And I don't want to talk about it anymore, so promise me you won't tell her, okay?"

"Okay, Carter," the small boy assures him. "But they might tell her."

"Who might tell her? Dillon and his friends?"

"No." Alex glances over his right shoulder toward the stand of trees. "Them," he says, pointing to a cluster of six large black crows.

12: Some kind of trouble

"This is it," Lily mutters. "I've had just about enough. *Enough!*"

She looks at herself in the mirror. "I'm strong, intelligent. I've had to fight for everything I've ever wanted. I have clawed my way through so much life shit to get to the top and I'm damn well going to stay on top."

She blinks back tears. "I had nothing but persistence, resilience and a never-give up attitude. I got here on my own. And no one, I mean *no one*, will take that from me. Ever. No fucking way."

And then she smiles. She never says the F-word to anyone but herself. But *damn*. It was liberating.

She stares at her cellphone and tells herself it's time to put an end to this bullshit that's been dominating her life over the past few days, infiltrating her every thought.

"Enough!" She says again, reviewing recent events that have caused her world to come apart at the seams. "I don't know what's going with Josh, but this stops now." She whispers, "It stops today."

She sighs. "Those bullies picking on my grandson make my blood boil."

She rubs her hand over her eyes. "And Alex. He's behaving like he's possessed. And these anonymous phone calls. I'm at my wits' end."

Picking up the phone and dialing the number for the local RCMP detachment, she's sure she can put an end to at least one of these problems. Tackling the bullying problem is the first item on her agenda.

"Liverpool RCMP," the woman's voice says. "Brenda speaking. How may I help you? If this is an emergency you should dial 9-1-1."

Listening as the woman gives her well-rehearsed spiel, first in

English and then in French, Lilly rolls her eyes. She knows this is normal protocol but it's one more delay and, in her current frame of mind, she's not happy about any delay.

"No, this is not an emergency, at least not right now, but I would like to speak with Corporal Cliff Graham. Is he in please?"

"I'm not sure if he's available right at this moment," the woman answers. "Who may I say is calling?"

"Lily Pittmann." She is feeling the stress slowly taking control of her life, crippling her and making her ineffective as a mother. "He knows me."

"Is the matter urgent, Ms. Pittmann?"

"Urgent enough that I would appreciate speaking with Corporal Graham about it, if you wouldn't mind getting him for me, please."

"May I ask to what this is pertaining to?"

"No. You may not."

Lily finds the woman's audacity off-putting. She knows that the receptionist may only be doing her job in trying to screen the corporal's calls, but she doesn't appreciate anyone prying into her personal business. "I will tell the corporal what I want when I speak with him."

"Just a moment, please."

Lily and Cliff go way back and she's confident she can talk to him about this problem as a friend, if not as a police officer. After what seems like several minutes, she finally hears the phone click on again.

"Lily?" She immediately recognizes Cliff's gruff voice. He sounds tired to her. "Sorry to keep you waiting so long, but I was on another line. Vandalism issues. The little bastards....I'm sure you've heard about them."

"I have and it's no problem. I know you're a busy man with lots on your plate so I don't mind waiting."

"How are you?" Cliff asks. "I haven't seen you and Josh in a while."

"I'm fine....We're fine," she lies. "And yourself? How about you?"

"Good."

"The family?"

"All good," Cliff answers. "Carly's about to graduate from high school in two days and I'm now feeling really old."

"That's called life." Lily says. "Time to accept it, Cliff. It's something we all have to face some day, but getting older surely beats the alternative."

"True enough," he chuckles.

Remembering Cliff's brush with death a few years ago, Lily knows it's a forced laugh. The heart attack was a close call for him, but he was smart enough to see it as a wake-up call and, as a result, changed his entire lifestyle.

"Seeing our children grow up and set out on their own is part of the cycle," she continues. "Trust me. I've already been there three times. We raise them as best we can and then we open the cage and set them free like little birdies. We send them out to face the big, bad world, but I don't have to tell you about the big, bad world. You see enough of that side of things every day."

"More than I care to, I'm afraid," he agrees. "So how are things with your current family?"

"Honestly?" She pauses. "Not so great right at the moment and that's the reason I'm calling."

"Something wrong, Lily?"

"Well." She swallows hard and then begins. "Carter, my grandson. He's now almost seven and he has been having problems with some bullies. That's why I'm calling. I'm wondering what I can do about it."

"That is a tough issue," Cliff says. "And unfortunately, it's a problem that seems to be getting worse every day. Is the bullying anything physical? Not that verbal isn't bad enough."

"A bit, I think. But you know kids. Carter won't tell me much. It's worse than pulling teeth from a horse."

"Kids don't like to talk about it when they're being bullied," Cliff says. "They think that talking about it will make it worse. Do you know who the other kids are?"

"I think so. One of them at least."

"What would you like me to do?"

"I'm honestly not sure, Cliff," Lily admits, wishing she hadn't felt compelled to make this call. "What do you suggest?"

"Do you think it would help if I talked to your grandson?"

Lily hesitates. "I don't want to scare him or make him think he's in some kind of trouble. He's already feeling bad enough because he thinks I'm mad at him for this, like I blame him for being the victim."

Cliff says, "Maybe if I talk to him, I can help him understand it's not his fault. He needs to understand unless someone stops them, bullies won't back off, and these things often end with someone getting hurt."

"Yes," Lily says. "Of course you're right, but I don't want to bring him to the detachment. That would be too hard on him and me."

"Agreed. I could drop by your place today if that would be okay with you. I'm tied up for the next few hours, but I have some free time later on."

"Okay, Cliff," Lily agrees. "If you think that's a good idea."

"You called me looking for help, Lily, so you must think it's time for someone to step in and help your grandson. The question is, do *you* think it's a good idea? Do you want me to talk with him or not?"

"Yes," she sighs. "Yes, I do. I know how this can turn out and I can't let it get to that point."

"Good. I think it's the smart thing to do. I could be at your place around one this afternoon, one-thirty at the latest. Will that time work for you?"

"That would be fine, Cliff. And thank you for understanding."

"Not a problem, Lily. Bullying is a serious problem and it's important to nip this thing in the bud before it escalates."

Then he says, "Is there anything else I can do for you?"

"What do you mean?"

"I mean, is there anything else bothering you?"

"Why would you ask that, Cliff?"

"I don't know," he says. "I just have a feeling. Do you need my help with something else?"

She hesitates, finally says, "I don't know....Maybe."

"What is it?"

"Can we talk about it when you get here? I don't really don't want to discuss it over the phone."

"Sure, Lily. I'll give myself a little extra time. But," he adds, "are you sure it can wait until this afternoon?"

"Yes. I'm sure it can. I'll expect you around one."

"Okay then. I'll see you then. Bye for now."

"Bye Cliff," she says. "And thanks for your help."

The call ended, she stares at the phone. *Damn. I hope I've done the right thing.*

"Nan?"

She hasn't heard the boys enter the den and she jumps at their sudden appearance in front of the desk.

"Hey, guys. You were so quiet and I was so deep in thought I didn't hear you."

"Was that Gramps?" Carter quickly asks. "Is he coming home today?"

"No, honey." She smiles at her grandson and son. "It was someone else. And no, Carter, Gramps is not coming home today. But I think we can expect him tomorrow."

"We thought you were coming out, Mommy," Alex says. "We wanted you to play soccer with us."

"I was on my way, honey, but I got delayed. Sorry." Lily smiles at them. "So how was the game? I watched you for a bit but then I got distracted with the phone call. You're both doing very well."

"Good," Alex answers, "but—"

"But he beat me," Carter says quickly. "He kicked my butt."

"Really?" Lily smiles at her grandson, who is at least twice as big as the tiny boy standing beside him, his deep, dark eyes peeking up over the edge of the desk at her. "He actually beat you?"

"Yup," Carter nods. "He's pretty good."

"I know he is." Lily winks at her son. "He's a pretty sharp little firecracker, aren't you, Alex?"

The tiny boy remains silent and Lily quickly picks up the vibe. "Everything okay?"

He shrugs.

"He's fine, Nan," Carter quickly says. "Just tired from the game, and hungry. When's lunch?"

"In about an hour." Lily keeps her eyes glued to her son. "Are you sure you're okay, Alex? Is there something you want to tell me?"

"No," Carter quickly answers again. "There's nothing."

"Carter," Lily says, glancing at the bigger boy. "Please let Alex speak for himself."

Turning her eyes back to her son, she asks, "Did something happen in the backyard while you guys were playing?"

Glancing to Carter and then back to his mother, the tiny boy finally shakes his head. "No, Mommy," he says, speaking softly. "Nothing happened."

"I don't know," Lily observes. "You two look guilty. Did you break something?"

"No," Alex answers.

"Did you lose the ball?"

He shakes his head.

"Did you have an argument?"

"No, Mommy," he whispers. "Nothing."

"See, Nan?" Carter says. "I told you nothing happened."

"Okay, if you say so," she says, giving up the questioning. "But if I find out something happened and neither of you told me about it then I *will* be angry. It's bad enough if something happens, but it's worse if you lie about it and keep secretes." Zeroing in on her son, she adds, "Right, honey?"

"Right, Mommy."

"Very well, then." She sighs. "You two run along and find something to do. I'll make lunch in a bit. And don't forget Hunter and his mom are coming by this afternoon."

Watching as the two boys scamper out of the den, Lily can't shake the feeling they were hiding something from her. She knows sometimes kids will keep secrets if they think the truth will get them into trouble.

Glancing at her laptop and the pile of reports resting on top of the oak desk, she thinks she really should do some work today, but quickly quits her programs and closes the computer cover. Collecting all the papers she has spread over the desk, she shuffles them into a neat pile and slides them into a file folder.

Work can wait, she thinks, rising from the padded chair.

Then she hears a commotion. It sounds as if it's coming from the back patio.

"Boys?" she calls out. "Is that you?"

When no one answers, Lily darts from the den and makes her way through the foyer to the bottom of the winding staircase. "Alex? Carter? Are you guys up there?"

"Yes, Nan," Carter immediately answers. "We're playing a video game in my room."

"Okay, honey," she replies, wondering what she could have heard on the patio. In the pit of her stomach she wishes the boys had been out there.

Moving from the foyer into the kitchen, she makes her way to the glass doors that open onto the patio and steps outside. She's sure she heard something out here and it sounded like a crash.

Scanning the patio, she sees the small table she uses for her drinks when she's resting out here has been knocked over, and the glass top is smashed.

"Shit," she says, scanning the backyard and pool area to see if someone might be around, but she doesn't see anyone. Someone had to knock over the table, and since it wasn't her and the kids were upstairs, she's convinced someone has to be prowling around.

"But who?" she mutters, returning to the kitchen and retrieving a broom from the closet. She knows the groundskeeper only works on Mondays and Fridays, so it wasn't him in the backyard.

I hate this, she thinks.

She brings the broom and dustpan to the patio and sweeps up the shattered pieces of glass before the kids come out and cut themselves. Maybe she should have waited in case someone was here, but she couldn't leave all the broken glass just lying there.

Try as she might, she can't shake the feeling something strange is happening around her house. She shudders as she glances up toward the back wing of the house where the boys' bedrooms are, and is startled to see six large black crows circling overhead.

"Shit," she whispers, feeling the breath catch in her throat.

"What do you want?" she asks.

The birds, their black feathers glistening in the bright morning sunlight and reflecting a purplish-green iridescent colour, swoop and glide over where she knows the children are playing.

"What do you want with my kids?" she says.

There is no answer. She carries the shattered glass into the kitchen, turning to close and then lock the patio doors behind her.

"Whatever you want, just leave them alone."

13: Nip it in the bud

"Hi Cliff," Lily says as she opens the huge oak door leading to the front veranda to greet RCMP Corporal Cliff Graham, the man who has been the commanding officer of the thirteen-member Liverpool detachment for over fifteen years. "Thank you for coming over so quickly. When I called this morning, I really didn't expect you would be able to come over so soon."

"You're more than welcome," Cliff replies, stepping into the brightly decorated foyer, a place he's been too many times in the past as he investigated cases over the years. *But all of that is now history*, he thinks. "Police sometimes get a bad rap for not caring enough, but it's just not true."

He removes his uniform hat and smiles at Lily. "We care....We care a lot, especially when kids are involved."

"I know you do." Lily closes the door behind him and listens for the click that confirms it's locked and secured. "I especially know how much *you* care, Cliff."

She leads him down the brightly-lit hallway he remembers as once being dark and dreary, the heels of her sandals clicking on the grey and white marble tiles. "I've known you a while and I know how much you care when it's something involving children. That's why I called you. I knew if anyone might be able to help, it would be you."

"Man," Cliff says, "I can't get over how much work Josh has done to this place. It's certainly changed a lot."

He takes in the expensive decorations that include paintings on the walls by artists with names he couldn't even pronounce. "This place looks nothing like it did when I first came here."

"That was his plan, Cliff," Lily says, reaching the door opening onto the den. "After everything that's happened here over the years, he didn't want anything that reminded him of the old man."

"I get it. That was some pretty nasty business."

"It sure was." She pushes open the door and motions for Cliff to go into the room. "I thought we could talk in here for a while. The children can't hear us in here so we won't be disturbed."

"Great. Where is Josh, anyway? If you don't mind me asking."

"Away on a business trip," Lily replies, following the officer into the den and then closing the door behind them. "He's due back sometime tomorrow."

"He goes away a lot, doesn't he? I mean, please don't get me wrong because it's really none of my business, but he does seem to be gone a great deal."

"That's the nature of his business," Lily quickly answers.

Cliff gets the message: she doesn't want to talk about her domestic partner.

"But if you don't mind, Cliff, let's chat before the children call me."

She motions toward a black leather sofa and love seat that face each other across a large, square coffee table Cliff thinks is made of mahogany, but he's really not sure since he knows very little about wood.

"Please have a seat."

"Sure," he says, sitting in the middle of the love seat while Lily sits across from him on the sofa. "I had small children once and I remember how demanding they can be when they want your attention."

He slips a small, black notebook from a pocket of his uniform, smiles at the woman and adds, "Tell me what's happening with your grandson, please. You've got my full attention."

"Is this an official report?"

"I'm not sure, Lily," he says, glancing at the notebook he's rested on his right knee. "I guess it depends on how serious the allegations are. Once you tell me something and I think it's serious enough to pursue it further, I won't be able to ignore it, especially if it could lead to charges."

"I don't know, Cliff." She pauses. "I'm not sure if we're ready for charges at this point."

"Why don't you let me decide," he says. "Just forget about my notebook and talk to me as your friend. Tell me what's troubling you and I'll make the judgment call. Trust me, Lily, if this is serious enough, this is the time to deal with it."

"I suppose, if you think it's serious."

"I've seen enough problems stemming from bullying over the years that I know what I'm talking about. As a matter of fact, a few years ago, I had to deal with kids bullying one of my own kids and it was messy business."

"Really? One of your children?"

Cliff nods. "Carly. It got so bad for her at her previous school we had to move her back here with me from Vancouver, where she was living with her mother. A group of other kids at the school had targeted her for whatever reason and it got so bad she started pulling back from everyone. She withdrew from everything she enjoyed doing and from her studies to the point it was making her a different person. We saw a major change in her and we were really worried she'd do something drastic so we had to help her deal with it."

"That's what I'm afraid of."

"Then let's nip it in the bud." He smiles. "Once it reaches that point, it's too late."

She nods. "Of course, you're right." She pauses. "I'm sorry, Cliff. Where are my manners? I didn't offer you anything. Would you like a drink or something to eat before we start? It wouldn't be a problem for me to get you something."

"Oh, God, no thanks, Lily. I just had lunch and I couldn't eat anything else. I've been working really hard to keep my weight under control and I keep close watch on my intake."

"And, I must say, whatever you're doing, it's working, because you look great."

Cliff recognizes his host is doing everything she can to avoid the real topic. "Thanks. But, if you don't mind, I'd rather get into this problem with your grandson. Okay?" He sees her immediately become tense. "Don't worry, Lily, I will be gentle."

"Very well."

She tells Cliff everything she's been able to find out about the bullying that's been happening.

"And you just found out about this yesterday?"

"Yes. Carter refuses to tell me anything about it, but apparently it's been going on throughout the whole school year. I was able to find out that much, at least."

"I see." Cliff makes a few notes on the ruled pad. "Well," he replies after considering everything she's just told him. "I really do think you should arrange for me to speak with your grandson. Can we do it today, since I'm here?"

Lily nods. "He's upstairs, playing. I'll get him in a minute. But first, if you have time, before we get to Carter, can I talk to you about something else that's bothering me?"

"Sure. What's on your mind?"

"You know, Cliff, I'm really not sure what's on my mind these days," she admits. "But it seems something strange is going on around here."

"How do you mean?" He cocks his eyebrow in her direction. He's been around long enough to know when someone starts a conversation by saying something strange is going on, it's actually a cry for help.

"Well," she starts, then hesitates.

"Go on, Lily," he urges. "Please tell me. I can see whatever this is, it's really bothering you but I can't help if you don't tell me what it is."

"Okay." She sighs heavily and then takes a deep breath. "Over the past two days I've been receiving anonymous phone calls and, truthfully, they're freaking me out."

"Do they say anything?"

"No." Her voice trembles. "They haven't said a word but I can hear them breathing and it's really getting on my nerves."

"How many calls?"

"Three. Maybe four."

"Do you have call display?"

"Yes, but it comes up as a 'private number' whenever they call."

"I see." Cliff pauses and thinks for a minute. "Isn't your number unlisted?"

"Not for the main number to the house. Just Josh's business phone. And I also get these calls on my cell. If it's a stranger, how would they get my cell number?"

"Hmm."

"What does it mean?"

"Not sure," Cliff admits. "But do you think it's possible it's these same kids that are tormenting Carter?"

"I had thought of that, but I honestly hope not. I'd hate to think of children doing something like that because, I've got to tell you, those calls are scaring the hell out of me. I don't like it one bit."

"I'm sure you don't."

"But that's not all. I also think someone's been prowling around the property."

He perks up as she continues.

"Last night, I found the patio doors open even though I'm sure I checked them before I went to bed and I'm positive they were locked. Then, just before lunch today, someone knocked over a little table out there and smashed the glass top."

"One of the kids, maybe?"

"No, sir." She shakes her head. "They were nowhere around and there was just us three in the house."

"This isn't good, Lily." Cliff says. "I'm glad you told me. You've done the right thing."

"So what do I do now? I have to admit it feels like something's off around here."

"What do you mean?"

"I can't explain it, but it just feels like something's not right." She struggles to fight back tears. "What do I do?"

"I will have a look around out back before I leave. When I get back to the office, with your permission of course, I will see if we can get a record of those calls," he says. "I may need you to contact your service provider to ask them for the records, but maybe we can trace them back to where they came from."

"Of course. Please do whatever you have to. This has just started but I have to tell you it's really got me spooked."

"I can see that. And for good reason. You can't let something like this go. There are a lot of crazies out there and you never can tell where something like this can lead. I mean, and please don't take any offence to this, it's not like you and Josh don't have a lot of valuable stuff around this house. You'd be a prime target for someone desperately looking for money, especially if someone knows Josh is away."

"I know, Cliff, and I admit I've thought of that as well. We do have alarm systems installed and I guess maybe it's time to start using them."

"I would say so."

"It's just the children get so scared when we tell them we have to use the alarms. The boys really think when we set the alarms it means someone bad is coming after all of us."

"I know how kids' imaginations can get the best of them, Lily. But if you have the means to protect your house and your family, you should use it."

"Of course, Cliff." She nods. "I know you're right."

"Please promise me that when Josh comes home you'll at least discuss this with him. I suggest you guys come up with a course of action just in case someone out there is really targeting this place."

"Now you're really freaking me out, Cliff."

He can tell he's got her on the verge of tears. "I'm sorry. I'm not trying to scare you. I'm trying to help you to understand that in this day and age, you can't trust anyone. People will stoop to any- thing to get ahead. I've seen people do some pretty extreme things for a whole variety of reasons."

"I'm sure you have."

"And you know all about that stuff, Lily," Cliff adds. "You've lived here a long time. You're aware of some of the weird things that have gone down in this town over the years. Sometimes their motives defy a simple explanation."

"Okay, Cliff," she says. "You've proven your point and I do thank you for your advice and your assistance. Please let me know what you need from me."

"You should contact the phone company and tell them what's going on," he says. "You can also tell them you've given the police permission to look into your records."

"I will take care of that today. Anything else?"

"Not right at this second."

He closes his notebook and slips it into the right-hand breast pocket of his uniform shirt. "Let me talk to your grandson and then I'll have a look around."

"Okay then." She rises from the sofa. "I will go and get Carter."

"And Lily." He also rises. "I know it's easy for me to say, but try not to worry."

"Sure."

She smiles, but Cliff can tell it's a forced smile. He pulls a card from his back pants pocket and hands it to her. "This has my private cell phone number on it. Feel free to call me even at night if something is going on and you need help. Or if you just need to talk."

"Thank you, Cliff." She goes to the large oak desk and slips his card into the top right-hand drawer. "I'll do that. Now, I will get Carter."

14: Targets

"Well, Lily," Cliff says as he joins her on the patio, "the conversation with Carter went exactly how I thought it would go. He denied everything and initially refused to implicate any of the boys who have been picking on him."

Lily sits silently, staring at the grass beneath her feet. She is completely at a loss for words. She's also not sure what to do about the situation but she desperately wants to help her grandson.

"Don't get me wrong. Carter didn't protect the boys out of any misplaced loyalty to them. He's a clever kid and he really didn't lie to me. He skirted the truth to avoid getting them in trouble to protect his own ass."

Lily half-smiles.

"He only did what others in his predicament would do when their instincts for self-preservation kick in."

Lily still isn't speaking, so Cliff continues. "Kids who are victims of bullies usually refuse to point fingers at their abusers. They believe if they do so they will be painting a larger target on their own backs, but in reality, they are only giving the bullies the freedom to keep on launching their attacks. It's a vicious, and often harmful, cycle leading to some very serious problems for the victims."

"He's afraid, Cliff."

Cliff nods. "He fears telling the police or anyone else about what's happening to him will only lead to more abuse from the bullies. I've seen it many times. However, I promised Carter I will do whatever I can to make sure it doesn't happen again. I will talk to the boys and their parents. Maybe I can make the boys understand the serious ramifications that bullying has on the victims. In some cases, once bullies understand they could face criminal charges, they back off and leave their victims alone."

But not always, Cliff thinks.

"I don't know, Cliff," Lily says, as if reading Cliff's thoughts. "Maybe you shouldn't do anything. At least not right now. I have read that some bullies think they are above the law and they'll push the limit while believing they can get away with anything."

"That's true. And these are the most dangerous kind of bullies I've ever encountered, but I promised I was going to help you handle this and I will. I'll call all the boys' parents and arrange a meeting which I hope will appeal to their sense of compassion. At the very least, maybe I can put a sense of fear in them if they see the police are now involved." He chuckles, hoping to lighten the tension.

"I'm worried about Carter." She respects Cliff, but now she wonders if she did the right thing by calling the police about this.

"I know you are and I'll do whatever I can to protect your grandson."

It took some doing, but Cliff had managed to convince Carter to tell him the boys' names, so at least he now has a place to start. "Now that I know what's going on, I'll keep an eye on things."

"And you'll keep me posted?" Lily asks as she heads to the patio doors. "I want to know everything that happens."

"Of course. You have my word."

"Okay then." Lily forces a smile. "Now, if you'll excuse me, I should go check on the boys."

"Sure. I just want to look around out here for a bit."

"Take whatever time you need. And, Cliff: thank you for doing whatever you can."

"Anytime, Lily," he answers as the woman disappears into the house. "I'll be in touch."

But for right now, as he squats on the massive flagstone patio at the back of the Goodwin mansion and studies the area where Lily told him she found the broken table, he's concentrating on trying to figure out if, as his friend believes, someone was actually lurking around here. He's looking for anything like footprints or perhaps something a prowler may have dropped.

Anything, he thinks, scanning the pool area.

If, in fact, someone has been prowling the property and making prank phone calls, Cliff knows those actions could be the start of something more serious, and he's hoping to find any clues that might help him better understand what's been going on. He knows Lily is frightened by what's been happening the past few days and he wants to help her, but he needs a lead.

Nothing. Completing his visual scan of the seating area where the table had been located, he moves on to the double glass doors Lily claims someone had gotten open last night even though she swears they were locked when she went to bed.

"Hmm." He kneels, observing what appears to be scratch marks in the white paint around the base of the brass lock and handles.

Could be someone used something to pick the locks.

He pulls out his cellphone and takes five quick photos of the marks. If this thing escalates into something serious, he knows this could be an important clue. He wants to have someone in forensics take a look at the doors before he reaches any conclusions, but the images could be useful.

But he knows it could also be nothing more than normal wear and tear. It's not unusual for homeowners to miss the locks and sometimes scratch the doors themselves with their keys.

However, given Lily has reported several calls and claims to have heard strange noises on the property over the past forty-eight hours, Cliff isn't about to dismiss anything without due consideration. He's been around long enough to know that, in police work, even the most obscure occurrence could be an important clue in any case.

Standing straight again, he scans the entire backyard property, with its breathtaking flower gardens of vibrant colours punctuated with well-groomed shrubs that make them look more fake than real.

Pretty big...and a lot of work. He shrugs. *Unless you can afford to pay someone to do the work for you.*

He realizes this is actually the first time he's been in the backyard, even though he's been to the Goodwin house many times in the past. Those visits have been on official police business for cases that tested not only his skills and resolve as a police officer but also his sanity.

Impressive.

He admires the pool and the surrounding cedar deck with a large hot tub and an outside shower area as well as a large water-fall, built of slate and granite, that spills into the pool on the furthest corner. Together, the features make the place a tropical oasis.

Nice.

He understands such a feature would cost big bucks, more than he could ever afford on his salary, considering he'll soon be helping to put two children through university. And, he cringes, after the end of this year he'll be doing it on his pensions and savings. He knows it won't be easy but he also knows it's time to hang up the badge. He's confident he's done his duty, often going above and beyond the call.

Still, he thinks, spotting a large growth of birch and maple trees lining the back edge of the property, *money can't buy you happiness*.

He knows that while the kind of money Josh Goodwin is ru-moured to have amassed in recent years could buy him anything he could ever want, it couldn't always buy the one thing most people covet—love.

Nor, Cliff thinks, as he leaves the patio and begins the walk across the closely manicured grass toward the stand of trees, *can it buy true respect or sincere loyalty*, two things most important to him as a police officer.

Reaching where the lawn ends and the trees begin, he pauses and takes in the surroundings. He listens as the traffic on the nearby street passes by. He's sure Josh Goodwin must be pissed every time he thinks about the town putting a road so close to his property, but he also knows Josh has enough money in the bank to build a ten-foot wall around this entire property, if he wanted to. He's actually surprised the rich man hasn't done just that. He's sure if he had a place like this, he'd do everything he could to pro-tect his privacy, but he also knows not everyone shares his feelings.

Spotting an area in the bushes that appears to be beaten down from on-going traffic, Cliff decides someone has recently come this way. Instinctively dropping his right hand to the holster on his hip, he sighs with relief, knowing his official force Smith & Wesson is within reach...not that he anticipates having to use it today.

But, he thinks while pushing through the bushes and following the path where it looks as if someone has recently trampled, *you just never know*.

As the bushes spring back into place behind him, Cliff pushes deeper into the stand of trees buffering the Goodwin property from the street. *Hot and stuffy in here. Not a good day to be trouncing through the woods.*

He follows the trail until he comes to an area where it appears some sort of scuffle has occurred.

"Hmm," he says to no one.

He stands still and scans the area, his eyes taking in everything in the immediate vicinity until they come to rest on a dark substance that appears to be covering three leaves on a low branch on one of the birch trees.

Approaching the substance, Cliff studies it for several seconds.

"Blood," he whispers. He makes a note in his black book of the exact spot where he's found it. He wishes he had brought some sample bags with him, but he honestly had not expected to find anything of consequence out here in the trees.

However, he thinks, stepping past the birch tree and following the trail, *this may be turning out to be more than I had suspected when I started this probe.*

Reaching the other edge of the trees several minutes later, Cliff stops and peers through the bushes. From this position, he sees the street and he knows it wouldn't be difficult for someone to park a vehicle here and then walk through these trees to get to the Goodwin property. To get to the house, all a prowler would then have to do is sneak across the lawn, which would be easy under the cover of night and with the shrubs and bushes providing protection.

Perhaps Lily has reason to worry, he thinks.

He makes his way to the street, stops and looks around.

Nothing.

He notes there are no other homes nearby, so if anyone wanted to get to the Goodwin mansion under the cloak of darkness to do God knows what, this would be the way to do it.

Scanning the gravel shoulder of the street, Cliff discovers several footprints in the loose rocks, but they look to be smaller than any adult's. He also sees tire tracks clearly made by bicycles, but he can't tell how many.

"Kids," he sighs. He tries not to draw any conclusions from what he's found, but instinctively thinks maybe much of this ruckus is the work of the same kids who are tormenting the Pittmann boy.

Still, he thinks, *this doesn't feel right.*

It's one thing for bigger kids to bully smaller kids, especially those who stand out, like a kid with an obvious weight problem, but it's a leap to think they would escalate to trespassing, harassment and break and enter.

It's possible.

He strolls along the roadside, his eyes scanning for anything out of the ordinary.

He has no doubt the bullies would come here to taunt the Pittmann kid. He's sure they would do that if they thought they could gain easy access to their target, but would they risk getting into more serious trouble by crossing the line to more serious crimes? He doesn't know the other kids involved in this scenario, so he's trying hard not to pass judgment, but he believes the bullying situation is more like a schoolyard vendetta than a possible home invasion.

He spots a tire track in the loose gravel where it's clear someone had parked a vehicle.

"No," he says, observing that from this spot he can't see the Goodwin house, which means no one in the house can see a vehicle if one were parked here. "This could be more than that."

He writes the location of the tire mark in his notebook, pulls out his cellphone and snaps a few quick images. *Just in case.*

He has now decided he will send an investigator back here to the Goodwin property to have a closer look at what he's found and to catalogue the clues he's discovered. He has no idea what's going down here, but his gut is now telling him something's up.

It could be nothing.

He turns to check out the surroundings and determines that he's now standing in one of the most isolated areas of the strip.

Or it could be something.

15: Watching us

Lily has known Samantha Henderson since high school, and while she would never have described the pretty blonde to be anything more than an acquaintance back then, she now considers her a very close confidante. Indeed, their friendship has grown strong in recent years, as if their mutual respect and admiration brought them together for some unknown purpose.

No one knows the two women have formed a close bond; not Sam's wife, the hotshot lawyer Kate Webster, and certainly not Lily's partner, the rich businessman Josh Goodwin.

It's not that either woman is ashamed of their friendship. In fact, just the opposite is true. They admire and care for each other very much. It's just that they believe having a special friend, with whom they can share things they can't or don't want to tell anyone else, gives them a brief reprieve from their real worlds. It's an escape. They both like having something of their own that no one else shares. Letting others know of their friendship, they believe, would be like letting everyone else into their private world, and they fear it might destroy their special connection.

They don't want that. They like being able to talk with someone who will not judge, someone who will simply listen and offer unconditional support. The women believe they don't have to justify their relationship to anyone. Instead, they let the world think they've developed a relationship primarily as a means to give their children friends to play with, which to them is merely a fringe benefit.

"So." Samantha sighs deeply and leans back, putting her feet up on the solid-blue lounge chair while pulling her Ray Ban sunglasses down over her eyes. In this position she can watch the children playing in the pool as they enjoy the tepid water that feels more like it's in a bathtub, just as Lily likes it.

"Tell me what's going on with you, Lily. You sounded really desperate earlier today. I worried about you all afternoon and couldn't wait to talk to you."

"Seriously." Lily hands her friend a margarita, the tequila-based drink they've both learned to love since Sam tried making them a year ago for a function she was catering at the local golf club. She holds her own glass and eases down on the lounge chair next to Sam. "I really don't know where to begin."

"You can begin by telling me what the hell is going on with you and Josh." Sam sips her drink. "Have you decided what you're going to do about him?"

"I think so." Lily nods.

"Whatever it is, make sure you'll be happy with the outcome," Sam advises. "I know you can't continue living with his lies and deceptions, but it's also clear you still care for the man very much. Tread lightly and think things through before you rush into anything, but in the end, you've got to do what is going to make you and the kids happy."

"Yes." Lily sighs and smiles. "Yes, I do. I love Josh very much, but I've finally reached my limit. I just have to know where he stands. If he really loves me like he says he does, then he'll put an end to all this cloak and dagger shit that's been going on for the past few years. If he doesn't, then I'm left with only one alternative."

"Just be sure. Once you give a man like Josh Goodwin an ultimatum, there is usually no turning back. He may feel like he's been boxed into a corner and react, no matter how much he loves you." She looks her friend square in the eyes. "Are you ready for the consequences?"

"I honestly don't know." Lily shrugs. "But I hope so."

Sam takes a sip of the cool liquid from the sleek and expensive glass. "So do I for your sake, but I want you to know I'm here for you whenever you decide."

"I know it's a gamble." Lily pauses. "But I think he'll see it my way. There's a lot riding on this decision."

"That's for sure." Sam senses it's time to change the subject. "You'll never guess what I heard today."

"God," Lily replies. She glances at her friend and smirks. She can only imagine what her friend had heard now. In her job as a caterer to many of the social functions around this town, Sam gets to talk with a lot of people, which means she also hears a lot of juicy gossip. "Now what?"

"It's nothing bad." Sam chuckles. "Actually, I heard today one of our long, lost friends may finally be returning to town."

"Really? Who?"

"Oliver Lewis."

"No way. I didn't think we'd see him around here ever again, not after everything that happened."

"Me neither."

"Truthfully, he moved around so much I had lost track of him."

"As did most of us," Sam says. "The only person I know of who had any kind of regular contact with him over is Charlie, and since he's Kate's brother, that's how I know so much."

"What's he been up to?"

"Mostly been travelling from place to place," Sam says and sips her margarita again. "Based on what Charlie says, it seems like Oliver was just kind of wandering the globe...kinda like a nomad. Maybe he was looking for his purpose. Whatever he was looking for, I hope he found it."

"Wouldn't it be nice to be able to do that?" Lily suggests wistfully, watching as her grandson splashes water at her son. But deep inside she knows she wouldn't want to give up what she has right here in Liverpool, despite the current problems she's having with Josh. "No responsibilities. Nothing to tie you down. No worries."

"I don't know. I suppose so. But I do like being close to home."

"Me too," Lily admits. "But if we went through what Oliver went through, maybe we'd see things differently."

"I guess so." Sam nods. The man almost died. I'm still not sure I fully understand what really happened with him. Charlie tried to explain it to us. He says the cancer went into remission, but that seems far-fetched to me. I mean, the man was on his deathbed for days and then, somehow, we're supposed to believe he miraculously gets up and walks away from all of that. Don't get me wrong. I'm happy it worked out for Oliver, because I like him very much, but it does seem hard to believe."

"It does." Lily nods. "But miracles do happen."

"Yes, they most certainly do....Especially around this town."

"Now who's understating the facts?"

"Touché." Sam winks at her friend. "We've all been witness to some pretty dramatic and unusual things."

"More than I care to remember," Lily says. "It's almost like our town has become the battle ground for the struggle between the forces of good and evil and most of the time, evil seems to win. We seem to have so much death and mayhem."

"That's rather cynical. Some good things have happened around here."

"I know." Lily shrugs. "That's the mood I'm in these days. It's hard for me to see a bright spot when my world seems to be dominated by the dark side."

"Okay, I know things aren't the best between you and Josh right now, but there's more to this. What else is bothering you?" Sam slips off her sunglasses and looks directly into her friend's face. "What gives? What's really bothering you?"

Lily hesitates.

"Come on, Lily. You know I'm here for you, but you've got to talk to me if you want me to help. You know how this works. Keeping it locked up inside won't change anything. It will only make them worse for you. So tell me what the hell's going on or do I have to beat it out of you?"

"Okay, okay. You win." Lily takes a drink. "For starters, I've talked to Cliff about the bullying problem Carter's been having and he's promised to look into it. I asked him to be discrete. I have no idea what that other kids might do if they think Carter told on them. He's terrified they'll come after him."

"You did the right thing, Lily." Sam nods. "Bullying is a serious problem no matter the age. You couldn't let it go."

"I know, but I hate involving he police. I'm not sure how Josh will react when he finds out," Lily says. "I know he likes Cliff and they seem to get along, but I've always had this feeling there was some sort of rift between them."

"How so?"

"I've never asked Josh about it, but I've always sensed a tension between them whenever they're together, so I'm not sure he will appreciate having Cliff poking around here." She pauses. "However, it gives me a little peace of mind knowing Cliff's close, especially now."

"Why especially now?"

"Just a second." Lily glances around the deck. "I want to make sure the boys can't hear us."

"Now you're really freaking me out. What's going on, Lily?"

Seeing the children are not within hearing distance, Lily whispers, "I think someone is stalking the house."

"What the hell are you talking about? Who?"

"I have no idea, but I'm really freaked out. I told Cliff about it." Lily swallows hard, catches her breath and then continues. "I told him I think someone's watching us."

"I want to know everything."

"I've been getting these anonymous phone calls and I have the strangest feeling someone has been prowling around the house and watching us."

"Jesus, Lily. Have you told Josh about this?"

"Not yet." Lily shakes her head. "I don't want to make him worry while he's away, but he's due back tomorrow so I'll tell him when he gets home. There's nothing he can do for us from wherever he is."

"I'd be so freaked out if it was me. I wouldn't be able to keep it from Kate," Sam admits. "I'd be jumping out of my skin if I thought someone was stalking me."

"Trust me." Lily's voice quivers. "It isn't easy."

"Do you have any idea who might be doing this?"

"Not a one. I can't come up with anyone who might do something so underhanded. I know Josh has enemies out there, as most successful business people make enemies at some point, but I can't, for the life of me, think of anyone who would be so devious."

"What does Cliff think? Are you in danger?"

"He thinks we should take it seriously. He wants me to start being extra cautious but I don't want to frighten the boys."

"That is a problem." Sam nods. "They do have an active imagination, but you have to find some way to skirt the issue with them." She pauses, then adds, "You don't suppose it's one of the children they're after, do you?"

Lily quickly raises her right hand in a gesture for her friend to not mention such a possibility. "I'm freaking out enough right now, so don't plant that idea in my head. I'd lose my mind if I thought the children were in danger."

"I'm just asking if you think it's possible."

"I suppose it is," Lily admits. "But I can't figure out why."

"For money." Sam is blunt. "Maybe someone is planning to kidnap one of the kids and hold him for ransom."

"Jesus, Sam! Don't even suggest that. The very idea of such a thing would kill me."

"People do know you guys have a lot of money. You don't exactly hide it." She glances around the immaculate property. "If this place doesn't scream 'rich people live here' then I don't know what does."

"God, Sam." Lily says as the tears begin to well in her eyes. She quickly wipes them away with her right hand before the children can see them. "Do you really think someone would target the children?"

"Desperate and greedy people will do anything." Sam is to the point. "You tend to look for the good in everyone, but some people can't be trusted."

"I know you're right."

"Are you going to be safe here until Josh comes back?"

"I hope so." Lily sighs heavily. "I'll make it a point of arming the alarm system before I go to bed and I'll sleep with the phone on my pillow."

"Do you have a gun?"

"Certainly not in my house."

"No?" Sam shrugs. "Me neither. Couldn't feel safe in my own

house if I knew there was a gun somewhere around."

"Josh doesn't like guns either," Lily says.

"I'm not sure I'd be much help if something were to happen, but would you feel better if I stayed over with you tonight? I think the boys would like that."

"I couldn't ask you to do that."

"Yes, you could," Sam insists. "Kate's gone out of town for a few days on a case, so Hunter and I are on our own tonight. We could make a party of it for the boys."

Lily hesitates. "Are you sure?"

"I am." Sam nods. "But I will have to be out of here by nine in the morning as this catering job is getting pretty close and I've got a lot to do to get ready for it."

"That's perfect, then," Lily says. "You can leave Hunter here with us until you're done. Then you won't have to worry about him while you're working. The boys can play in the pool and you can take all day if you have to."

"You wouldn't mind keeping him?"

"Not in the least. He's really not a problem when he's here with Carter. They get along really well. They have their moments every now and then, but then again, who doesn't?"

"Okay, then. Thanks for doing this." Sam's smile melts Lily's heart. She loves doing things to help her friend. "I'll run home and get some things for both of us and we'll have a fun night."

"Indeed we will," Lily agrees. "Indeed we will."

16: Six crows gold

"Finally." Lily flops into the dark green armchair across from Sam. She's tired and needs a break.

Children, she thinks, kicking her sandals off her aching feet, *can really wear a person out.*

She had a difficult time getting Alex to settle down this evening. She thought they'd have problems with the older boys, but they were so exhausted from playing all day they actually went to sleep right away. But not Alex. He's usually a good sleeper, but for some reason tonight he fussed for hours and demanded Lily's attention, which she gave unconditionally.

"Hey there." Sam smiles. "Thought you got lost. I've been entertaining myself with this scrapbook of old photographs and papers I found on the coffee table. I hope you don't mind."

"Sorry about that," Lily whispers. Her eyes are closed. "And no, I don't mind. Pictures are made to be looked at."

"Did you finally get him settled down?"

"Yes." Lily sighs heavily while rubbing her temples with the tips of her slender fingers. "And thank God he did because I'm just about played out. I don't know what's gotten into him lately. He just hasn't been himself and I'm getting worried."

"How so?" Sam asks, her right eyebrow instinctively rising along with her curiosity.

"Well..." Lily doesn't really want to tell her friend what's been going on. Then she shrugs and says, "For starters, he's suddenly developed this fascination for crows."

"Oh God," Sam says, automatically feeling her body becoming stiff and tense. "You did say crows, didn't you?"

"I did," Lily nods. "And on top of everything else, he's really the last thing I need to be worrying about right now."

"You've got that right." Sam smiles at her friend, but not in a funny way because she knows this is nothing to laugh at. "What are those black devils up to now?"

"I just don't know, but it does look like they have taken a keen interest in Alex. I've seen them myself. It's very creepy the way they just appear out of nowhere and hang around. It's kind of like they're keeping an eye on him. I know it sounds weird, but that's how it feels to me: like they're watching him."

"I don't find that weird at all. I've experienced that sort of thing myself with those freaking birds, so I get it," Sam assures her friend. "How many are we talking about?"

"Six. There are always six."

"You know what that means, don't you?"

"I do. Six crows gold," Lily says, her voice low and tense. "But I have no idea how to interpret any of that."

"You know," Sam says. "I'm not sure you should be looking for the literal translation. After years of observing the crows around here, I've concluded the message with these birds usually has a hidden meaning. Sometimes it's so obscure you have to be a detective to figure it out."

"You've lost me," Lily admits, studying her friend's face for clues to explain what she is talking about. "I don't understand what you mean."

"I'm just saying you shouldn't get caught up in the literal meaning," Sam says. "Most people, when they think of gold, they think of money or jewellery. But it's possible there's another meaning— some sort of hidden message."

"Ahhh. Now I get you. So what else could it mean?"

"I don't know," Sam admits, slowly shaking her head. "What else could have a significant connection to something gold?"

"The one thing that immediately comes to my mind is anniversaries. Fiftieth anniversaries are celebrated with gold, but I can't think of anything significant in that regard and certainly nothing that would have anything to do with Alex."

"Birth dates? Special events?"

"No. Nothing comes to mind."

"Well, if fifty is the golden number and six crows means gold, then there's the mystery, isn't it?"

"Or, it could be nothing." Lily says. "It could be just our imaginations running wild with far-fetched speculations and old myths. Maybe all the stories of the crows being involved in supernatural behaviour around this town are nothing more than old wives' tales."

"You really think so?" Sam deadpans. "After everything that's happened around this town over the years involving crows, you're willing to dismiss this out of hand?"

"I'm trying really hard not to get caught up in paranoia, but I will admit it's not easy," Lily concedes, her eyes narrowing as she contemplates her friend's words.

"And for good reason. If I were you, I would keep a close watch on Alex."

"For sure," Lily says, pushing herself out of the armchair. "And the crows."

"Of course," Sam nods. "And the crows."

"It's getting late, but I think I'd like to have a cup of tea before turning in," Lily says, heading from the family room toward the kitchen. "Want one? It will only take a few minutes."

"Sure," Sam says. She slides to the edge of the sofa and pulls her long, straight blonde hair back behind her ears. "Before you go though," she adds, turning her attention back to the scrapbook lying on her lap, "I want to ask you about this book. What is it? I don't recall ever seeing it before."

"It's been around here forever," Lily says. "It belonged to my great, grandmother, but normally it's up on the shelf over there." She points to a built-in wall unit that holds books, collectibles, ornaments and nick-knacks in various shapes, sizes and colours. Sam knows these items are important to her friend, so she's surprised she hasn't seen this book before.

"But," Lily adds, "I'm not sure what it's doing down off the shelf. One of the boys must have had it out and forgot to put it away."

"It's fascinating," Sam says.

The book has a worn red-velvet padded cover and dozens of heavy black pages made of construction paper. Each one is covered with photos, newspaper clippings and notes in various handwriting styles, suggesting that several different people had their hands on the collection over the years.

"Yes," Lily agrees, returning to sit beside Sam. "My great grandmother, Clara Underwood, loved to collect photos and newspaper clippings. She was into scrapbooking long before scrapbooking was in vogue."

"I love looking at old pictures," Sam says. "I can't believe you've never shown me this before. Why did you keep it hidden?"

"I wasn't hiding it. I guess it just never crossed my mind you would be interested in a bunch of old stuff about my family," Lily says. "I just assumed no one else would care to see them."

"Are you kidding?" Sam slowly flips the pages, taking a few seconds to study each picture secured to the pages. "They're priceless," she continues, examining the changing fashions and hairstyles. "I could spend hours looking through these things. You can learn a lot about your past by looking at old photographs."

"I suppose." Lily sighs and shrugs. "I never thought much about it. This old thing just landed here after Grammy died. Truthfully, I've hardly looked at it."

"Wow," Sam says, suddenly stopping at one page and scanning a picture of a handsome man in his late twenties or early thirties. He poses next to a horse and looks like he's holding a newspaper in his hands, although it's difficult to see it clearly. "Wow," she says again.

"Wow what?" Lily asks, craning her neck.

"Wow this," Sam says. She turns the book sideways so Lily can get a better look at the photo. "When was the last time you looked at this book?"

"I don't know. I guess it's probably been a few years. As I said, I've never really had much of an interest in that kind of thing. Whenever my mother started talking about the family and stuff, I'd usually glaze over."

"Take a good look at this photo," Sam says placing her finger next to the image of the man. "Do you see it?"

"I'm not sure."

"Yes you do. You must."

"Okay," Lily answers. "If you say I must then I must."

"Do I have to spell it out for you?"

"Yes," Lily fires back. "Obviously you do. Just tell me what I'm looking at, for God's sake."

Sam moves her finger to the face of the man. "Look at his eyes and the features around his mouth and nose. If that's not Alex standing there, then I'm not sitting here having this conversation with you."

"What?" Lily peers at the photo. "No way."

"Yes way," Sam insists, sliding her finger over the image. "*That* man right there in *that* photograph is exactly what your son is going to look like when he's that age."

Studying the picture for a while, Lily finally says, "Oh my God." She hesitates and then continues, "I do see it....There is a striking resemblance, but it's normal, isn't it? After all, he was our ancestor."

"I guess so," Sam says. "But it's really uncanny. Who was this man?"

"There," Lily says, pointing to the names someone has jotted in ink at the bottom of the page. Reading through the names, she finally says, "It's Jonah Ross."

"Jonah Ross," Sam repeats. "Who was Jonah Ross? According to the date on the newspaper he's holding, this photo is over one hundred years old, at the least."

"Clearly, since my great grandmother kept meticulous records, he must be one of her relatives. She was an Underwood by marriage," Lily says, sliding her small frame off the sofa. "Let me see if we can figure this out."

"Where are you going?"

"I'm getting Grammy's family Bible." Lily makes her way to the built-in shelving units. "Everything I could ever want to know about my mother's side of the family is written in that old book. If he's a long-lost relative then he'll be listed in the Bible."

"Hold it, Lily," Sam says quickly. She flips through several more pages. "Come back here and look at this. Now I'm really freaking out."

"What?" Lily asks, returning to the sofa.

"Take a good look at all these pictures," Sam says, handing the book to her friend. "Pay very close attention to the backgrounds."

"Jesus," Lily sighs heavily, flipping through the pages and studying all the photos as she goes. "What in the name of all that is holy?"

"See them?"

"I do." Lily nods. "Crows. There's crows in the backgrounds of all these pictures."

"What the hell is that all about?"

"I have no idea," Lily answers, glancing at her friend. "But now I am officially freaked out, too."

17: Coming clean

"It's time to do it," Josh whispers, even though he's alone. "I don't want to. But I have to. If I don't, we're as good as dead anyway."

He has finally accepted it is time to come clean with Lily. His body aches with the lead weight on his shoulders pulling him down. Unless he tells her, he knows their relationship will die a painful death.

Ever since she gave him the ultimatum, he hasn't been able to think of anything else. The bird hitting the window this morning was the final straw.

Josh accepts he is a superstitious person. He got it from his mother, crazy woman she was, but he can't shake the feeling someone—or something—was sending him a message with the sparrow, and since he's struggling with the ghosts of his past, he's concluded the message must be related to that.

Tossing in the hotel bed and staring at the ceiling, he's tried to close his eyes, but no matter how tired he is, sleep eludes him. He can't erase Lily's words from his memory. They've been beating around in his head all day. He could tell she's finally reached her limit, and even when he called her earlier this evening, as he does every night when he's away, he could sense she was being distant.

Even when he asked her about the kids, it seemed she didn't want to talk to him. He knows it hurts her deeply when he disappears, as he's been doing ever since they first got together several years ago. He also accepts that, without her love and support during those difficult times, not only would his business be in shambles today, he would most likely be struggling to maintain his sanity.

If in fact I am, he thinks, throwing the sheets off his body and sitting up. Swinging his feet over the edge, he rests his elbows on his knees and drops his head into his hands.

Is this really sanity? What am I going to do, he wonders. Either way he goes with this, he runs the risk of losing the woman he loves and maybe even being cut off from the boys.

That would be devastating. He stands up and grabs the remote control from the night table. He flicks on the television. *If I can't sleep*, he thinks, *I may as well be watching something*. He's got more than twelve hours to go before his flight, but he knows he will never fall asleep this night.

The colour picture blinks on to an episode of the classic sitcom, "Everybody Loves Raymond". *Doesn't matter if it's an oldie but a goodie.* This was one of his all-time favourite shows. Besides, he only wants the TV on for company since the silence in the room is driving him crazy.

Tossing the remote on the bed, he goes to his jacket and rummages through the pockets until he finds the pack of cigarettes he bought earlier today. So far he hasn't opened them, but he can't resist any longer, even if this is the no-smoking section of the hotel.

He quickly peels off the plastic wrapping, tosses it into the trashcan next to the scuffed brown dresser he's sure must be a clone of every other dresser he's seen in every other hotel room he's ever been in. *Mass produced. Cheap but workable chipboard.*

Sliding a cigarette out of the package he makes his way to the window and opens it a few inches. He tells himself he should not be doing this, but his resistance is low. It's been many years since he's had a cigarette and he hasn't craved one in a long while. When he was in school, and immediately after graduating, he smoked up to two packs a day, but he kicked the habit well over a decade ago. Lately, however, he's been craving the soothing relief of the nicotine. Bowing to the pressure, he instinctively bought a pack of smokes when he paid for lunch this afternoon.

His guest couldn't believe that he actually bought cigarettes, and he couldn't believe it either.

What the hell. He slips the tip of the brown filter between his lips, bringing the small, yellow and blue flame to the cigarette and dragging hard.

Jesus, he coughs, as his airway and lungs immediately react to the intrusion by the foreign and caustic substance. He places his mouth close to the open window and quickly exhales, watching as the smoke leaves the room and immediately dissipates. Now he knows why he quit smoking in the first place.

Puffing on the cigarette again, he wonders about the best strategy he should employ when delivering news that could ultimately change the life of the woman he loves.

Damn. He spins around, looking for some place to dispose of the cigarette. *This is so gross. What am I doing?*

He heads to the bathroom and runs the lit end of the cigarette under a steady stream from the tap, then tosses the barely-burned cigarette into the toilet and flushes. Watching the water as it swirls around the toilet bowl and eventually swooshes down the drainpipe, pulling the cigarette with it and heading to a destination God knows where, he suddenly feels dizzy.

He flicks off the bathroom light and returns to the room, where he plops on the bed and stares blankly at the television screen. He watches as Raymond and his wife, Debra, are engaged in a heavy discussion about something he's done that pissed her off. He's not really tuned into the show so he has no idea what they're arguing over, but it's clear to him she's letting him have it with both barrels and he can't help but wonder if that's what it's going to be like for him when he finally tells Lily his big secret.

Will she understand? Will she forgive me? Or will she be really angry and kick me out?

Sighing heavily as he watches the two actors on the television, he decides he wouldn't forgive Lily if the roles were reversed. He's sure of that and, if he's being honest with himself, he really doesn't expect her to do it either.

He grabs the remote control, pushes the red button, and watches the screen turn to black. *Maybe she'll leave me and take me for everything I have. I wouldn't blame her if she did.*

He grabs the pillows and punches them a few times in a futile attempt to fluff them up, in hopes he can catch a few hours' sleep after all before he has to leave for the airport.

He certainly hasn't given Lily any reason to stay with him—or to trust him. But maybe, he hopes, the love for her children will be more powerful than the hate and loathing he's sure she'll have for him once he springs the truth on her. And maybe, he thinks, her love for her children will transfer to him because she'll understand the boys need him in their lives.

How in the world could anyone be prepared to hear such a horrendous secret? He closes his eyes and tries to force himself to fall asleep.

She can't. His eyes pop open and he stares up the ceiling again. *She can't and that's the problem.*

One Day Before

Vernon Oickle

18: Never tempt fate

It's almost dawn and the house is deathly quiet. In fact, it's so quiet that Lily finds it eerily unsettling. She swears she could hear the beating of a butterfly's wings if one were to flutter by right at this moment. The only sounds she can hear are those her own body creates—her steady breathing, the beating of her heart and the voices in her head.

She knows she should be sleeping, but her mind is too busy to rest. She's tossed and turned for the last four hours, as her thoughts dwell on events of the past few days. She can't shake the feeling that all these events are leading up to something, but to what, she has no idea. It's like a heavy weight is resting on her chest and she feels lost and helpless. She hates feeling this way.

Secrets.
Lies.
Bullies.
Anonymous callers.
Prowlers.
Crows.

It's the last item that worries her most, as it appears her son is somehow involved with these mysterious black birds that have suddenly appeared and have come to roost on their property.

Are they here for Alex?

While she admitted to Sam the sudden appearance of the six crows hovering around her house and seemingly honed on her two-and-a-half-year-old-son has her worried, in truth, she's actually terrified they bring bad news with them. She's heard all the stories about the crows being messengers of death and the harbingers of doom, but she hates to talk about those old beliefs because she fears talking about them will somehow make their warnings come true.

"Never tempt fate." Lily whispers, remembering her great-grandmother Clara Underwood warning others when the family would visit the old woman. She may have been but a young child when they'd go to the ramshackle house out on Gull Island Road, but she was old enough that the words were forever seared onto her memory.

Lying here this morning, staring out the window as the early hints of sunrise peak over the horizon—the spectacular mix of red, orange and yellow light just starting to crack the blackness of the early summer night—she can hear the old woman's words right now in her head just as clearly as if she were sitting here on the edge of the bed with her.

"Never dare the crows to make good on their warnings, because if you provoke them, the black birds will do just that," she hears Clara saying. "They are powerful and all-knowing and when challenged, they will never back down. They know things. It's wise to always take them seriously."

She would punctuate her warning by adding, "Now you mark my word, or else."

Lily remembers her own mother dismissing Clara's talk as the ramblings of a senile old woman who had "taken leave of her sanity," but after everything that's happened around this town over recent years in which the crows have seemingly been in the mix—if not the actual cause—she's really not sure. It seems to her that there may have been some truth to her great-grandmother's warnings, and Heaven help those who choose to ignore such signs.

It's those thoughts that are now keeping Lily awake. She wonders why the crows have suddenly taken an interest in Alex.

Why him? What makes him so special? Why now? Why six? What does 'six crows gold' really mean?

And the photos Sam and she discovered in the old scrapbook earlier tonight. *What could they mean? Who was Jonah Ross?*

Perhaps a relative I know nothing about, she speculates. *If so, what's his story? Why had she never heard of him before? Was the family keeping him a secret and if so, why?* She'd admit that his uncanny resemblance to her son is a little more than disturbing.

Shivering despite the warmth in her bedroom, she thinks it was downright frightening that the older face of her young son was staring back at her from the page of old scrapbook and through the eyes of a man who lived at least a century ago.

What about the crows that were in the backgrounds of many of the photos, but not all of them? What could it mean? Why would some be chosen and others not? Are these people special? If so, what makes them special?

More to the point, she wonders, pressing her head deeper into her thick pillows, *how does all of this relate to Alex and the crows that are now hanging around the house?*

Is he special? How? Why? Is he in danger? How can I protect him?

"Stop it," she tells herself, turning her head and staring up at the stark white ceiling, which she can just faintly see in the darkness. "You can't do this, Lily Pittmann," she says. "You can't let yourself get caught up in paranoia."

But, she admits, *I've long considered Alex to be special in many ways.* She's seen him do things no child his age should be able to do and she's sensed he has abilities he hasn't even discovered yet, but she's never wanted to admit anything to herself and she's never told anyone about her suspicions—not even his father.

She's staring at the ceiling, lost in her thoughts when she's suddenly interrupted by the soft click of her bedroom door opening.

"Mommy?" It's her son's unmistakable soft voice.

"What's wrong, baby?" She bolts upright and stares at the small boy standing in her doorway.

"I heard them again."

"Who, honey? Who did you hear?"

"The black birds."

"What did they say?"

"They said I should not be scared."

"Scared of what, honey?" she asks, reaching for the lamp on the bedside table and snapping it on. "Come on up here," she adds.

She waits for him to crawl into bed with her. As he pulls his tiny body up and slides under the covers next to her, she asks, "Did they say what you shouldn't be scared of?"

"No," he whispers, snuggling under her left arm.

"Maybe you were dreaming," she suggests, running her bony fingers through his black hair.

"No, Mommy," he insists, closing his eyes. "I was awake."

"Couldn't sleep?"

"Nope."

"Me neither," she tells him. "But try closing your eyes and going to sleep now. It's still really early and we can't get up yet because we'll wake up everyone else in the house."

"Okay." He sighs and she can feel him trembling next to her.

"Alex?" she asks, her voice soft and tender. "When you hear the black birds talking to you, what's it like? Is it like when I'm talking or like Carter is talking to you?"

"No," he quickly answers, glancing up at her with his dreamy dark eyes. "I hear them inside my head."

"Like you're thinking it?"

"I don't know, Mommy." He shrugs. "I just hear them and they tell me things."

"Do you hear them a lot?" she probes, realizing pushing him for too many details might actually frighten him more than he is already.

"Just sometimes." She can tell he's starting to dose off. "Can I go to sleep now?"

"Yes, baby," she whispers, leaning in and kissing him gently on the forehead.

As she turns to reach for the lamp, there's the unmistakable sound of shattering glass.

"Mommy?" the small boy next to her cries out.

"I'm here, Alex," she quickly replies, hugging his tiny body close to hers and trying hard to disguise the fear in her voice. "It's okay. There's no need to be afraid. I think something must have just fallen over down stairs and broken."

"What?" he asks.

Then there's a light knock on the bedroom door. "Lily? It's Sam." She was sleeping in one of the guest rooms further down the hall. "Are you awake?"

"I am," Lily answers. "Come in. Alex is here with me. He couldn't sleep."

"Did you hear that?" Sam asks, pushing the door open just wide enough for her skinny body to slide through. "It sounded like something glass breaking."

"Yes," Lily says. "We heard it."

"What should we do?" Sam sits on the edge of the bed, next to Alex's feet. "Should we call the police?"

"I don't know," Lily answers, her voice shaky. "I don't want to call them if it's nothing. If there comes a time when I really need them, they might not come."

"It has to be something. Maybe it's related to what we talked about earlier. We both heard glass shattering and glass doesn't break for no reason."

"Of course not," Lily agrees. "But maybe I left a window open and the breeze blew the curtains and knocked something over."

Sam glances toward the window. "I don't think it's breezy out there." Turning back to face her friend, she adds, "Besides, do you remember having any windows open? Doesn't an air circulator control this entire house? Why would you have windows open after what you told me earlier?"

"I don't know." Lily shrugs, pushing the sheets off her lean body. "I've got to go check it out."

"Where are you going?" Sam asks, the urgency in her voice betraying her fear. "You should stay here and we should call someone."

"It sounded like it came from downstairs, so I'm going to have a look," Lily says, sliding out of bed. "You stay here with Alex while I check it out and I'll be right back."

"That's a stupid thing to do. What if someone's down there?"

"I'll be fine. There's no one down there." Lily slips into her housecoat and makes a beeline to the bedroom door. "I won't be long."

"Lily," Sam says. "Please don't go down there."

Ignoring her plea, Lily cautiously moves down the dimly lit hallway, her breath catching in her throat as she steps carefully along the beige carpet. She'd be lying if she said she wasn't scared as hell that she could be walking into danger. Common sense tells her she should phone the police and let them check out the origin of the shattering glass, but, despite the possible danger, she feels compelled to carry out her own investigation.

Reaching the bedroom where Carter and Hunter are sleeping, Lily turns the knob, pushes the door open just a crack and peeks inside. Finding the boys sleeping soundly, she pulls the door tight again and cautiously continues down the hallway to the sweeping staircase.

Pausing briefly to gather her courage, she then begins her slow descent, stepping carefully as the early morning light filters in through the side windows, defused and fractured by the older glass kept during the home's extensive renovations. She has no idea where the noise came from, but she decides she'll start with the kitchen. Ever since Alex told her he found the patio doors were unlocked the other night, she's been feeling paranoid about them and she wants to make sure they're locked tight.

Reaching the bottom of the stairs, she makes a right and enters the large, well-equipped kitchen with all the modern appliances and conveniences anyone could ever want. Josh offered many times to hire someone to cook for the family, but Lily refuses. Cooking and baking are two of her favourite pastimes.

Normally, she loves her kitchen, but this morning as it basks in the eerie shadows of the quickly-retreating darkness of a restless night, she feels uncomfortable and wary entering the room. Taking a deep breath and stepping slowly into the kitchen, she can sense a heavy pall settling over the room.

"Come on, Lily," she whispers to no one. "This is crazy. Get a grip, girl." She breathes heavily. "Get a grip."

Stopping at the light switch, she's about to flick them on when she pauses. *What if I'm not prepared to see what might be here?*

"That's crazy," she shrugs, swallowing hard and flicking the light.

As the darkness runs away, Lily quickly scans the room, studying every nook and corner and looking for anything out of place. "Nothing," she sighs in relief.

Her eyes wander to the double French doors leading to the back patio and her gaze comes to rest on a windowpane that appears to be shattered. "What the hell?" she says, her breath catching in her throat.

She cautiously steps around the large island cupboard with its counter-top gas range. She's not really sure what she's expecting to find—maybe a rock or something that may have been tossed through the window—but instead she sees a large bird sprawled on the white and grey tiles. With its wings spread wide as if it is still in flight and with the pool of blood circling its black body, it's an ominous sight.

"Jesus," she says as the churning in her stomach threatens to make her vomit.

She knows the crow is dead.

19: A warning

"Maybe it's a warning," Sam says softly to Lily over the tea they're having in the family room while the children eat cereal and fruit at the breakfast bar in the kitchen.

"From whom?" Lily asks, sipping her tea. It burns during the journey to her stomach. "About what?"

"I don't know." Sam shrugs and stares blankly at Lily. "But think about everything going on around here over the past few days." She pauses, takes a sip of tea, studies her friend and then continues carefully. "You've got to admit it's pretty freaking weird. We were just talking about crows last night and you were telling me how strange they've been acting lately. Then one of the damned things crashes through your kitchen window and kills itself. If you ask me, it's a pretty big coincidence."

"Is it?" Lily shrugs, peering at the pretty blonde woman over the top of her teacup. "Like I told you, I've been seeing a lot of crows around here lately and maybe one of them got disoriented in the dark and somehow managed to crash through the window. You're suggesting it was intentional, that the crow killed itself for some reason..." She pauses. "I just can't accept it."

"It would become disoriented now? Why? Come on, Lily." Sam sighs forcefully. "Don't you think that's a bit of a stretch? When was the last time you heard of a crow crashing into someone's window? They're too smart to do that."

"Stop it, Sam," Lily says, fighting back tears. "You're not helping."

"I'm not helping?"

Lily immediately regrets the comment. "I am sorry," she quickly says. "I didn't mean that the way it sounded. I know you're only concerned."

"And I know you didn't mean to bite my head off." Sam smiles. She's not angry at her friend's comment because she understands Lily is actually terrified about what may be going on. "But I'm worried about you and the kids. What if it's not safe for you guys to stay here?"

"We're safe, Sam."

"How do you know that?"

"Look at this place," Lily answers, glancing around the large room. She offers her friend a smile. "It's literally a fortress. No one can get in here if we don't want them to get in. Besides, Josh will be home by mid-afternoon, so we'll be fine."

"Your fortress didn't keep the crow out last night," Sam says, her eyes narrowing at the thought of the bird smashing through the door window. "What if that was just the beginning?"

"It was a freak accident," Lily says, shaking her head. "I didn't have the alarms set last night because we had guests. If we had set them off accidentally, you and Hunter would have been scared to death. We've done it before and it's not pleasant. Trust me. I didn't want to do that to you and Hunter."

"I don't know, Lily," Sam says. "I think you should call Cliff and at least talk to him."

"And tell him what? That a crow broke into my house last night?"

"You're making jokes?"

"I'm not," Lily insists, reaching out to take her friend's hands. "I'm trying to be realistic. I can't call the police about this because it's not a criminal matter. It's a freaky act of nature and I've taken care of it. I cleaned up the body and got rid of the mess before the boys got up. I've put plastic over the broken glass and when Josh comes home he'll take care of it. Now," she squeezes Sam's hands gently and smiles softly, "you go upstairs and get yourself ready for work. Didn't you say you had to get started early today?"

"I did." Sam nods, pauses and then adds, "But are you sure you'll be okay?"

"Yes. We will be perfectly fine right here. This is our home. Besides, where else would we go?"

"To my place. You could take the boys and go there until Josh comes home."

"I'm not about to let some birds chase me away from home."

"Come on Lily. You need to take this more seriously."

"You go to work and have a good day. I'll take care of your son. He'll be fine. If anything changes, I will be in touch right away."

"Fine. You win," Sam says. "If you're sure about this."

"I'm positive." Lily nods and then takes a sip of her tea. "Now get your ass to work before I throw you out."

"Okay. Okay." Sam chuckles, rising from the green sofa. "It will only take me a few minutes to get ready and then I'll disappear, but call me if you need me for anything."

"Take as long as you need today and make that place look really nice for all the graduates on their big day tomorrow. Hunter is fine here until you're finished."

Sam gives Lily a gentle hug. "I don't know what I would do without you."

"You don't have to worry," Lily whispers in her ear. "I'm not going anywhere."

Sam darts from the family room, stops at the breakfast bar to give Hunter a hug and then disappears to get ready for work. Lily suddenly feels an icy shiver run up her spine.

"Shit," she whispers, quickly glancing around and checking out the windows, but she can't see anything or anyone.

Unable to shake the feeling she's being watched, she sits her cup on the coffee table, pulls herself out of the huge green arm chair and moves to the row of windows that look out onto the sprawling backyard. She looks for any sign someone might be lurking around there, but she sees nothing.

"Damn," she whispers as the goose bumps rise on her arms.

"Nan?"

"God," she says, quickly spinning around. "You scared me half to death, Carter." She chuckles nervously. "I didn't hear you behind me." She swallows hard. "Sorry, honey. What do you want?"

"We're done eating," the boy answers. "Can we go outside to play now?"

"Yes. But Carter—" She stops him before he can leave. "I want you to stay on the patio today."

"But Nan—!"

"No, Carter." She raises her right hand to tell him to stop whining before he even gets started. "I said I want you to stay on the patio. You've got lots of toys and games you can play with there, or you can go for a swim, but don't leave the patio. Do you understand?"

"But we can't play soccer on the patio, Nan."

"Sorry, but you heard what I said. If that's not good enough for you, you can stay inside and play upstairs. It will be your choice."

"Okay." He sighs, realizing it's no good to argue with his grandmother.

As he turns to leave, she adds, "Gramps will be home this afternoon and then he'll do something with you guys."

"Promise?"

"I promise." She smiles while thinking it's one thing for her to make a promise but another for Josh to keep it. However, she's pretty sure that, when he comes home today, Josh will pretty much do anything she asks him to, just to keep her happy.

Turning to look out the bank of windows once again, she thinks about his homecoming. She's looking forward to him being here because she'll feel safer, but she's actually kind of dreading his arrival, because she knows at some point they are destined to have a conversation, and it may be a conversation she won't like.

Scanning the yard once more time, she sees a sudden movement near an azalea bush on the edge of the property. "Crows," she says, quickly spinning around. "Carter," she calls just as the three boys are getting ready to open the patio doors. "Stop."

"What Nan?" Her grandson responds more sharply than he probably intended.

"Watch your tone, young man."

"Sorry," he answers but this time more calmly. "Yes, Nan?"

"I've changed my mind. I don't think you should go outside just now."

"Why?" the trio ask in unison.

"Because," she answers, approaching the patio doors, reaching past the boys and turning the locks. "I said I'd like for you to stay inside for now. Please, no arguing. Just go upstairs and play for a while, okay?"

"Okay," they reluctantly concede, turning and then speeding down the hallway as only three young boys can.

"Okay, you crows," Lily says, reaching for the blinds and dropping them over the patio doors.

She makes her way around the kitchen and family room, closing the blinds over all the windows as she goes. "Please go away. I really can't deal with you right now."

20: Alexandria Gorham

With the blinds pulled down snuggly over the windows to keep out prying eyes, Lily feels like she's in a prison. She hates feeling trapped inside her own house, but she's too afraid to open the windows, let alone step outside. Sam's been gone for about two hours, and the last time she checked on the boys, about half an hour ago, they were upstairs in Carter's room, engaged in a virtual soccer tournament on the video system her grandson got this past Christmas.

She doesn't like her children to play video games, but she's okay with the sports games since they require the boys to move around. She knows video sports is no substitute for the real thing, and she'd like to open the doors and set the boys free, but given what's going on right now she believes it's the only option. Like it or not, she's decided she is not allowing the children to play outside today.

She knows it's a beautiful, sunny summer day and the children would enjoy the backyard and maybe even a swim in the pool, but until Josh comes home and checks things out, they are all staying put inside, where she knows everyone will be safe.

In the meantime, she thinks as she stacks the last of the cleaned breakfast dishes in the cupboards, *I may as well keep myself busy cleaning up the house. How can one adult and two little boys create such a mess?*

It's been a few days since she's really done any housework and she's allowed the place to get the best of her. *In truth*, she thinks, as she glances around the large room, trying to figure out what chore to tackle next. *I haven't felt like doing much of anything*. Her mind has been preoccupied with thoughts about crows, prowlers and bullies.

Lily has always taken pride in keeping a clean and tidy house, and she's a little ashamed of the mess things are in right now. Even when she was holding down a full-time job and raising small children, she always managed to get everything done. She refuses to let herself get slack at this point.

I will get this place straightened up before Josh gets here, or I'll give it a damned good shot, at least, she tells herself, kicking into high gear.

With the kitchen in order, she sets her sights on the family room, which basically just needs a bit of picking up and dusting as, despite what the name implies, it's one of the rooms in the large mansion that gets very little use. *Truthfully,* she thinks, zeroing in on a stack of magazines and books on the coffee table—the old scrapbook of photos with the red cover among them—*it's really wasted space.*

But when Josh renovated this sprawling estate he inherited from his father, he insisted they needed a family room. However, since he spends most of his free time in the den or the bedroom or out on the patio, and she spends most of her time in the kitchen or bedroom or on the patio, they never seem to use the space.

Perhaps, she thinks, *when the boys are older we'll use it more than we use it now.* But she doesn't think so. If anything, she knows the older the boys become, the more out of sight they're likely going to be.

Why would they want to hang out with their friends in front of their parents? she wonders, shuffling the magazines into a neat pile and placing them strategically in the centre of the coffee table for easy access should anyone want them, although she can't imagine who that would be right now, since she isn't expecting company and she's already read them.

Soon time for the recycling bin for you guys, she thinks while eyeing the scrapbook with the photos and newspaper clippings.

"And you," she says to the book as if she were speaking to an actual person. "You caused me to lose a lot of sleep last night." She picks up the book, sitting on the edge of the large green sofa and caressing the red cover like she's rubbing the head of a child.

"You've given me a real headache."

Flipping the book open to the first page, Lily scans the black and white photos that date back more than a century and depict men, women and children doing a variety of things or standing still in formal poses. She's amazed at how meticulously these records have been maintained over the years. While she knows her great grandmother, Clara Underwood, was the last person to have the book, she has no idea who started the collection or through whose hands the book may have passed before it ended up in her keeping.

At first, she didn't even want the scrapbook or the Bible or anything else the old woman left for her, because she had no use for them. But now, the historical material is rather fascinating, if not even disturbing, in an odd sort of way, when thinking about all the people whose images are captured here, people long since dead, buried and all but forgotten. *These books provide a complete history of my family dating back to the late-1700s.* She knows some historians would be envious of the detailed records.

In monetary terms, the book is worth nothing, but it gives her goose bumps when she considers its personal value. *Without the people pictured in this book*, she thinks, *I wouldn't be here today.*

That reality causes her body to tingle as if her nerve endings have suddenly become overly sensitive. She feels tiny electrical charges coursing over her body. *Without these people, my children would not have been born to continue the family bloodline.*

Ironic, she thinks, flipping through the book. *When I was pregnant with the twins, it was actually Josh who suggested the babies' names—Andrew and Alex.* He had been aware of the folklore surrounding the woman named Alexandria and that's why he liked Alex as one of the names. She is sure he had no idea the original settler who had come to Liverpool and started her family bloodline was actually *her* ancestor, but she knew. She's not sure why she's never told him that tidbit of family history, but it just didn't seem important back then. *Now*, she thinks, *I'm not so sure. Maybe it is important after all.*

She shivers. For a second it seems a little unsettling for her to think some of the blood that flows through her veins actually flowed through the veins of all these people depicted in these photos, as they are all related to one woman who arrived in the new world over two and a half centuries ago. As one of the original settlers of Liverpool around 1760, this woman planted the seeds that started this entire family tree, leaving a legacy filled with myths and traditions that have become one of the town's greatest and most endearing legends...of the witch known as Alexandria Gorham.

She remembers her great grandmother's stories of Alexandria Gorham. According to her, the Gorham family was one of the first to settle in these parts. They were important people back then, rich and powerful. But Alexandria eventually became an outcast and people turned on her and shunned her.

It's not really clear what, if any, crime the young woman had supposedly committed, but, according to legend, in the early years most of the locals considered Alexandria a saint. They said she could work miracles and did impressive things to help people when they faced hardships. She cured sickness, helped to mend animals that had fallen ill and tended to the destitute when they needed a hand. Others in the settlement came to view her as a witch. It appears that that particular faction had more control over the early settlement and they made her an outcast.

According to the story Lily recalls hearing throughout her childhood, something tragic happened when Alexandria was in her late teens or early twenties and many of the settlers blamed the young woman because they believed her power was responsible for attracting evil to their village. Eventually, the townspeople drove her away. The legend says Alexandria went into the woods one day and just vanished, never to be seen or heard of again. It was shortly after her disappearance that reports of unusual crow behaviour began appearing in the town's history. The black birds have been wreaking havoc in Liverpool since then.

According to the information on the pages of the family Bible, Alexandria Gorham had a child, a boy, whom another wealthy family raised in secret. The boy grew up and played a major role in the town's early history. Eventually, he found a wife and had children of his own, some of whom were prominent in the town's affairs. The family bloodline continued down through the generations. Based on the family tree in the Bible, Lily is a direct descendant of Alexandria Gorham.

Even though it is all intriguing, it is the photo of Jonah Ross that *has* now captivated her. Stopping at the scrapbook page that has the man's image, Lily studies his features and shivers.

It is amazing, she thinks, *how much Alex looks like this man.*

"But who are you?" she says aloud. She can't shake the feeling something is missing. There's a piece of this puzzle that isn't quite clear, and she knows she needs to find it.

Setting the book on the sofa with the page opened to the photo of Jonah Ross, she decides there's only one way to solve this mystery. She makes her way to the built-in shelving units to get Clara's family Bible with the black leather cover. It is on the fifth shelf, where she keeps it with the scrapbook and other valuable books she has collected over the years.

How the scrapbook got to the coffee table the previous evening, she has no idea, but that's not important to her now. She's more interested in the Bible. She knows if there's any question about anyone in her family tree, the answer *has* to be in that book.

She pulls the book from the shelf and she studies the gold-embossed words. "Holy Bible," it says. "KJV. King James Version."

"Okay, Old Woman," she sighs, carrying the old book back to the sofa and opening the leather cover. "Let's see if you can tell me who this Jonah Ross person is."

Turning to the first page she sees the first entry in the book is Alexandria Gorham. The name is written in beautiful flowing form in dark, black ink. Under the name it says, "Born 1749: Thatcham in Berkshire {Great Britain}."

There is no date of death, because no one knows when Alexandria died...*or whatever in the hell actually happened to her,* she thinks. However, she sees someone, at some point over the years, added a footnote in pencil: "Came to Liverpool 1760."

That would have made Alexandria a girl of eleven when the Gorham family arrived on these shores. But Lily wonders what could have transpired after that to have elevated the young woman to both the status of saint and the devil.

What could have she done that made her an outcast? What was so bad the villagers drove her out of town?

"There's a lot of history to be told in that story," she says to the empty room, her eyes dropping down the page, skimming over the names and dates written in various handwriting styles and in various inks and pencil.

Flipping through the next few pages, she eventually finds the entry for her great grandmother, Clara Underwood; only she is first listed as Clara Marie Ross. Beside the woman's name is…

Lily stops reading.

"No way," she whispers, reading the next entry several times. "No way."

She swallows, the saliva going down hard, as her throat suddenly feels dry and hot, like a desert. She stares at the entry in the Bible for several minutes without a thought in her mind. The detail she's found on the yellowing page leave her dumbfounded.

"Jonah Alexander Ross," she finally reads aloud. "Twin brother of Clara."

She glances back to the scrapbook and studies the photo. She feels her heart beating faster and her breath coming harder.

"No way," she whispers. "Jonah Alexander Ross. Twin."

Turning her focus back to the Bible she looks at the name again.

"That's impossible," she says, thinking it's the weirdest coincidence she's witnessed in a long time.

Turning to the next page, she finds her name and then those of her children, her three oldest with Tom Pittmann and her youngest, Alex Goodwin—a twin.

"This is too much," Lily says.

She has never even heard of Jonah Ross, let alone knew he was a twin to her great grandmother.

"Wow," she sighs. Then, as if struck by a thought, she says as if speaking to someone else in the room, "Alexandria, how many descendants are in your direct bloodline?"

She flips back to the first entry and counts those who follow.

Minutes later, as she reaches the final name in the Bible, that of her son, Alex, she stops short. She's struck by another strange coincidence.

"Fifty," she says with emphasis. "Fifty," she repeats, as if making a point to someone even though she's still alone in the room. "Alex is the fiftieth descendant of Alexandria Gorham. Fifty...as in gold... the golden child."

Then it hits her. Goose bumps break out over her arms and run up her spine, lingering on her back between her shoulder blades. "Six crows gold," she whispers, her voice cracking as the tears stream down her flushed cheeks.

Feeling her head spinning, she glances around the room, looking for anyone or anything to talk to. She needs to talk to someone. She needs answers.

She wishes Sam were here and thinks about calling her, but decides it's not a good idea. *Why get Sam worked up? This is crazy. It's nothing but superstition.*

"Six crows gold," she says again. She slams both the Bible and scrapbook closed with loud thuds. "What the hell does *that* mean? What's the connection with Alex?"

She quickly makes her way through the kitchen and to the patio doors. Reaching the blinds she had drawn earlier this morning, she takes a deep breath and parts two of the slats. Forcing herself to remain calm, she puts her face close the blinds and peers out.

There, on the patio, she sees them, lined up on the railing in a straight line as if they are soldiers waiting for orders that will send them into battle. But instead of battle, the black birds are staring intently at the house. It's as if they are maintaining a quiet vigil— perhaps for the crow that died here last night—or, she thinks, it also appears as if they are on guard duty.

She can't be sure what they are doing but she's sure they see her.

Quickly snapping the blinds closed, she backs away from the doors. "Six crows gold," she whispers. "My God." She swallows hard. "It is Alex."

Stepping further away from the doors, she cries, "What do you want with my baby?"

She sobs, calling out to the large black birds roosting just out-side her house, "Leave him alone. Go away. Please..."

21: Golden child

It has been hours since Lily discovered that the roots of her family tree, that lead all the way to her son Alex, might actually mean he's in some kind of danger, but she has *no* idea what it all means. She's tried telling herself it's all her imagination, but she's not doing a very good job of convincing herself.

"It's all a coincidence," she tells herself again, while making lunch for the boys and cleaning up afterwards.

Just my imagination running wild, she thinks as she sits in the big green chair, watching the large black hands on the antique grandfather clock as they tick toward three o'clock. She's loved this floor-to-ceiling clock since she saw it when she visited the Goodwin mansion for the first time. It was a few years ago but she remembers the visit well, especially the beautiful clock. Its flawless, red cherry wood confirms it to be somewhere around one hundred and twenty-five years old and the beautiful grain caught her eye right away.

Josh explained that his father purchased the clock from the proprietor of a local hotel, who had gone bankrupt and was eventually forced to close the business. The man needed some quick cash to help pay off his mounting bills and, according to Gerald Goodwin, the owner sold the handsome clock right out of the hotel lobby for one hundred dollars.

Gerald had a knack for finding treasures like this. Recognizing the bargain that it was, he fished into his billfold, pulled out a fresh hundred-dollar bill and placed it in the man's hand. An hour later, the clock was sitting in the foyer of the Goodwin mansion, where it remained until Josh moved it into the family room during the renovations. According to some appraisals, the clock is valued anywhere between eight and eleven thousand dollars.

But today Lily is not worried about its value. Today, she's more interested in the time on the clock's big face, because when Josh phoned from the airport about two hours ago, he told her he would be home around three o'clock.

"Come on Josh," she says under her breath, glancing at the three brass pendulums through the large glass door on the bottom of the clock cabinet. *Where the hell are you?*

"Come on. Come on," she says, over and over.

Ever since this morning when she read the names in the Bible, studied the old photograph of Jonah Ross and put two and two together, she's been a nervous wreck. She's tried to remain calm, but she thinks if he doesn't walk through the door right now, she's going to come unglued.

The thought that the crows have targeted her son for some reason is more than she can accept, and she has no idea what to do about it. For the first time in a long while, she wishes her great grandmother Clara were still alive. She's sure the old woman would know what all of this meant. She's sure Clara would be able to help her understand the connection between her son and the crows.

But with the old woman gone, there is no one she can talk to about this. She's not even sure if she'll be able to explain it to Josh without sounding like a lunatic, but she knows she has got to make him understand their son is in some sort of danger.

He'll think she's crazy; she's sure of that. But he's lived in Liverpool his entire life and he too has seen some amazing things involving the black birds, so she hopes he'll be able to find the answers for which she's searching.

He has to, she thinks, as she hears a car coming up the driveway, *for our son's sake, not mine.*

"Finally." She darts to the front window. Pulling apart two of the slats in the blinds that are still drawn tightly, she peers carefully outside and feels adrenaline rush through her veins. "Josh," she says, letting the blinds go closed again and running from the family room, through the foyer, to the large oak front door.

She throws the door open and greets Josh just as he's about to slip his key into the brass lock.

"Lily," he reacts with surprise. "You scared the shit out of me. What are you doing? Are you really that happy to see me? After what you said to me?"

"Relieved is more like it," she answers, waving him quickly inside. "Come on. Come on. I need to talk to you right away."

"Well, hello to you, too," he says, entering the foyer and sitting his bag on the granite-tiled floor.

"Yes, Josh," she says, stretching up to give him a quick peck on the right check. "Welcome home."

Then she spins and heads for the family room. "Now come in here, please. We need to talk."

"Already?" Josh says, reluctantly following the wiry redhead into the large room next to the kitchen. "I haven't even had time to unpack and you want to have this conversation now?"

"Not *that* conversation," she shoots back." She flops into the green armchair that all but swallows her up. "We have more important things to talk about right now."

"Okay, Lily," he says. He sits on the sofa across from the chair. "Now you're really starting to freak me out. What's going on that's got you so worked up, and why is it so dark in here?"

He glances around the room. "Why do you have all the blinds closed? It's a beautiful sunny day outside yet you've got everything barred shut. What's going on?"

"A drink," she answers, quickly standing and bolting to the bar. "That's what we need. Scotch okay?"

"A Scotch would actually taste good right about now. I'm tired after the trip. But you don't usually drink in the middle of the day. What gives?"

"I need something to calm my nerves." She grabs two stout crystal glasses from under the bar, reaches into the bar fridge for crushed ice, and then pours them each a healthy shot of Jack Daniels.

"Easy, honey," Josh cautions, seeing the amount of liquor she's just poured. "Are you trying to get us drunk?"

"Maybe I'm already drunk," she says, carrying the Scotch back to the sitting area and thrusting a glass toward him. "And you better drink this, too, because after I tell you what's been going on around here, you're going to wish you *were* drunk."

"What are you talking about, Lily?" he asks, accepting the Scotch and taking a sip as she takes her seat in the armchair. "You're really freaking me out."

"You should be freaked out." She chases her words with a large gulp of Scotch. She pauses and then, as the tears well in her green eyes, she blurts out, "Because I think someone or something is trying to kill our son."

"What?" Josh stares at the woman he loves, as it appears she's lost her senses. "What the hell are you talking about?" He sits the Scotch on the table. He's decided he'd better not drink after all. This situation might demand he has a clear head. "Who on earth would be trying to kill Alex? He's not even three yet. Have you lost your mind?"

"Nope." Lily gulps again and shakes her head. Then, in a low, gravely voice, quickly explains, "It's the crows. They're after Alex. He's number fifty in the book and they want him."

"Christ Lily," he says. "Now you're babbling. Crows. Book. Fifty. What are you talking about?"

"Six crows gold, Josh," she insists, her voice becoming forceful and tense. "Six crows gold. It all makes sense. Six crows means something gold. He's the fiftieth ancestor of Alexandria Gorham, which makes him the golden child. Don't you understand? In mythology, fifty is the golden number. It's the magic number. It's special. It can do all sorts of things. *Alex* can do all sorts of things."

"I really don't understand what you're talking about," Josh says, taking a large drink. He's decided he needs alcohol after all. "You need to slow things down a whole lot and tell me what's going on."

"Fine," Lily says, gulping down the last of her Scotch and getting up from the chair again. "But first let me get another drink."

22: Crow feathers

"So you're telling me six crows are after Alex for some ungodly reason?"

"Yes," Lily whispers. She wipes tears from her eyes with the back of her left hand. "You haven't been here, Josh. You haven't seen what's been going on for the past few days. It's been really creepy and I'm scared."

"And so you told Cliff Graham?"

She couldn't get a read on whether he's mad at her for talking to the RCMP officer she's known for years and would trust with her life, or if he's hurt on some level because she hadn't told him any of this while he was away. But whatever he's thinking, she hopes he knows she must have felt she had no other choice but to go to the police.

"Not about the crows," she says. She doesn't know whatever happened between Josh and Cliff, because they have never discussed it, but she knows they don't care much for each other. "Just about the bullies who are harassing Carter and that someone may be prowling around here. I thought I needed help because I didn't think the kids and I were safe."

"What did he say?"

"He said we should take it seriously and he'd look into it." Lily sighs. "Don't be angry at me for talking to him. I was scared. I was afraid someone was lurking around the property and I have no idea why or what they might be planning. What would you have me do? It's not exactly a secret we have money and you know what some people will do when they want money."

"No." Josh shakes his head; his smile is forced. "I'm not angry at you. Of course you did the right thing. If someone is prowling around the property then we have to find out who it is."

"So what do we do now?"

"I don't know."

Josh pulls himself from the sofa and leaves the family room. Making his way through the kitchen, he pauses at the patio doors and studies the plastic Lily has taped over the shattered windowpane. "This is where the bird came in?"

She has followed close behind. "Yes."

"I'll get it fixed today," he says, turning the locks and throwing open the doors.

"What are you doing?"

"Looking around."

He steps out onto the patio and closes his eyes for a moment to bask in the mid-afternoon sun. "It's a beautiful day. We shouldn't be cooped up inside. The boys should be enjoying the fresh air and sunshine."

"Yes they should, but what about the crows?"

"What crows?" he says, glancing around the sprawling backyard. "I don't see any crows. As a matter of fact, I don't see anything except the birds and the bees, and a beautiful pool calling for us to have a swim."

"Don't patronize me, Josh." Lily spins around and heads back into the kitchen. "I'll let the boys know you're home and tell them they can now come outside with you."

"Lily. I didn't mean anything, honey. I believe you. I honestly do, but we can't become prisoners in our own house."

She walks away without acknowledging him and disappears down the hallway leading to the foyer.

"Well, fuck," he mutters. "That didn't go exactly how I'd planned. Fabulous way to fuck things up." He snorts. "If this is how our future discussions are going to end up, things are worse than I thought."

Moving to the centre of the patio, Josh studies the surroundings. He soaks up the beauty of the gardens where Lily spends a lot of her time, feeling the freedom that comes with this property he considers his sanctuary. He felt trapped in the congested city and he's glad to be home, even if he met some sort of conspiracy theory.

He knows he should have been more supportive of Lily. He can see she's terrified of something. He also knows when someone raises alarms about strange crow behaviour around this town, he should take it seriously. He's seen too much over the years to dismiss anything about those black birds.

"Crows," he whispers, strolling around the patio, rubbing his hands over the cedar railings and marvelling at the bright colours Lily has coaxed from the gardens. He looks at the furniture and runs his eyes up the side of the house, painted white with black trim and window sashes.

Breathing deeply and taking in the crisp, clean air, he's searching for anything that might be a clue as to what has been going on in his absence. When he sees one large black feather in a bush near the patio doors, he feels the adrenaline rush through his veins. Right away, he knows Lily's assessment of the situation is right on target.

"Jesus." He retrieves the feather, holding it up in front of his eyes and examining the sleek, aerodynamic wonder of nature that helps the crows remain aloft. The mere presence of one solitary crow feather sends shock waves through his nervous system. "What do you bastards want?" he whispers.

Josh has had his own experiences with the powerful black birds. Only one other person knows of his connection with the crows, and he's sure that person would never divulge his secrete. The idea that anyone would use a crow as a murder weapon may seem far-fetched, but he knows the powerful birds are intelligent and loyal. They will do anything for the right person, if they feel a special allegiance to them or they know the person has been wronged. He has seen that firsthand.

Though the day is hot for June, Josh feels ice cold as fear snakes through his body. It's been a long time since he did the unspeakable—the dreaded secret he hides from his wife—to gain control of the entire Goodwin empire, but now Josh fears maybe the crows have come back for revenge. *Maybe,* he shudders, *they've come back to collect on my debt. And maybe*—he dreads the thought—

they're after Alex as some sort of payback.

It's possible I'm giving the black birds too much credit, but I don't think so. He knows Lily is right when she says they should never underestimate the power of the crows.

He's about to check around the backyard for any other clues when he hears the unmistakable sounds of young children rushing toward him. He spins around just in time to see Carter and Alex run out onto the patio. Their friend Hunter is lagging behind. Obviously, he doesn't share the other boys' excitement that Josh has returned and taken their attention away from him.

"Gramps," Carter yells with excitement. His eyes are opened wide and his smile is as broad as a barn door. "You're home."

"Yup," Josh laughs, kneeling and giving his grandson a tight hug. He rubs his large hands through the boy's black hair. "And I'm glad to be home. I missed you a lot."

"We missed you too, Gramps," the older boy says. "Can we go in the pool now? Nan won't let us play outside today."

"Sure. Go get your swimsuit on. I'll stay out here with you guys while you play."

Breaking away from his grandfather, Carter dashes back to Hunter and says, "Let's go change. We can go in the pool now."

So much for the homecoming, Josh thinks as he notices his other son appears to be hesitating near the patio doors.

"Everything okay, Alex?" he asks. He is still kneeling on the cedar decking, expecting his son to come and greet him with a hug.

The young boy nods.

"All right then," Josh says calmly. "Come over here and give your dad a big hug. I haven't seen you for a few days and I missed you."

The boy takes one step forward but quickly pulls back. He shakes his head no.

"Okay then," Josh whispers, pulling himself up. "I'll just come to you."

Alex stands firm near the patio doors as his father approaches.

"Are you okay, son?" Josh asks, kneeling in front of the tiny boy. "Are you afraid to come out here on the patio?"

The boy nods.

"Why?"

The boy shrugs.

"Are you afraid of the black birds?"

The boy shakes his head no.

"If it's not the crows, Alex, then what's wrong?" When he doesn't get an answer, he asks, "Why won't you come outside? I'll be right here and I promise everything will be okay. There's nothing to hurt you."

The boy shakes his head again.

"Do you want to stay inside?"

"Yes," he whispers, backing up through the doors and into the kitchen.

"Okay, Alex," Josh says softly. "If that's want you want, but I wish you would tell me what you're afraid of."

Alex blinks but says nothing.

The air in the backyard is suddenly shattered by a deep, guttural cackling Josh recognizes right away.

"Crows," he says, quickly standing straight and throwing his gaze around the backyard and patio. "Where are you?"

"There." Alex points toward a cluster of rhododendron bushes that have just lost their blooms.

Following the boy's finger, Josh locates the birds. "How many are there, Alex?"

"Six," the boy answers without hesitation. "There are six of them."

"That's what I was afraid of," Josh mutters.

He watches the black birds prancing around the yard near the bushes, strutting and preening as if they owned the premises. "Let's just wait in here for a minute, Alex."

"Why, Daddy?" the boy replies. "They're my only friends."

23: A hard pill to swallow

Sitting in his brown, leather swivel chair, Josh studies grain patterns in the large antique oak desk. He couldn't swear to it, but he's certain someone *has* been going through his things. And while he can't prove it, he's also certain it was Lily.

Who else would it be?

Quickly grabbing the handle of the desk's bottom right-hand drawer, he tugs and sighs in immediate relief that it's still locked. He knows Lily is curious about what he's been up to. He also knows she has been snooping around looking for answers about where he goes when he disappears three or four times a year, but he fears she will never understand, and he wouldn't want her to see what's in the drawer. The information in there would pretty much blow the lid off of everything he's worked so hard to hide.

If she's going to learn his secrets, he thinks it's best he be the one to tell her, instead of having her stumble across information she may not fully comprehend. Out of context, the material in his drawer could destroy him. *I really should find a better hiding place before that stuff ends up in the hands of the wrong person.*

It's just that he never thought Lily would stoop to nosing around his private things, but now it's clear her curiosity has gotten the best of her. Just as soon as he has the opportunity, he'll dispose of this information. Then it can't bite him in the ass. *I should have just gotten rid of it a long time ago.*

But it soon won't matter anyway, he thinks.

"How are you doing?" Lily asks as she enters the den and sets another glass of Scotch on a ceramic coaster at the corner of the dark oak desk. "Thought maybe you could use this."

"Thanks," he nods, smiling warmly at her. "I think I do."

"Listen." She moves to the black sofa in front of the fireplace at the other end of den. "I'm really sorry for the way I was acting when you came home this afternoon. You didn't deserve to walk into all of that mess." She pauses and studies his reaction before continuing. "Just because I've been on edge doesn't give me the right to be a bitch."

He retrieves his Scotch and joins her on the sofa. "I get it." He takes a sip and savours the smooth liquid in his mouth for a second before swallowing. "I understand why you were so worked up. We all know what those birds are capable of. We've seen it firsthand. But we have to try to keep our heads glued on straight, or else they win."

She nods. "Of course; you're right. It's just that I really felt I was close to the end of my rope, and didn't know what to do about it. And," she pauses, swallows hard and then continues, "I admit I was angry with you because when I really needed you, you weren't here. You were off on one of your secret missions."

"I can explain."

She raises her right hand to stop him. "Before you get all pissed off at me for bringing it up again, let me just say I am in no mood for an argument tonight. If you don't want to tell me what you've been up to, I get it. I don't like it, as you know, but I'm too tired and upset to push the issue right now."

"Okay," Josh replies, sipping his Scotch again. "How are the boys?"

"They're finally sleeping. They've both had a busy day, and after Sam picked up Hunter, they both showered, played a few video games and conked out. Even Alex went out with little trouble tonight, which surprised me because he's had a difficult time getting to sleep these past few nights."

"Why? Usually, he's a good little sleeper."

"Usually," Lily nods, "but not recently...not since you've been gone."

"That's strange."

"A little bit."

"So," Josh smiles at her, "here's the thing. I want you to know, no matter what happens and no matter what I tell you, I love you very much. If I had to, I would give up everything I own to protect you and the boys. You three are the most important things in my life. You must know that." He looks into her green eyes. "Tell me you know that."

"You're scaring me, Josh," she whispers, looking away.

"No, Lily." He takes her by the chin and gently turns her face to his. "I need to hear you say it."

"Okay," she answers, the tears welling in her eyes. "I know you love me—us—and you will protect us with everything you have."

"That's right. Now," he swallows hard, "I also must ask if you are prepared to hear some truths that will most likely change your perspective about everything you think you know about me."

"What are you saying?"

"Even though you may think you want to know the truth, you are not always prepared to hear that truth when it finally comes out." He reaches for his Scotch and takes a long sip. He wants to give her time to digest what he's saying. "Once the truth is spoken you can't take it back, and it can change your perspective."

"I don't understand."

"The truth. It's sometimes more difficult to deal with than accepting that we all have secrets. We all have them, Lily. You. Me. The kids. Your friend, Sam. Cliff Graham. Everyone in this town. Our secrets are part of what makes us who we are. The question is, do you think you can handle a truth that could change your world forever, a truth that will most certainly change how you look at me?"

"What have you done, Josh?" she asks, wiping her eyes. She is shivering. "Have you done something bad? Something illegal?"

"I have," he admits. "Lots of bad things. In order to tell you where I go when I disappear, I also have to tell you what I've done. Are you ready for the truth?"

"Are you having an affair?"

"God, no," he quickly fires back. "I would never cheat on you. I love you too much to do anything like that. I wouldn't even consider looking at another woman, let alone climbing into bed with one. You must know that. I want to marry you, not run around on you behind your back. That would be the ultimate betrayal and I would never do that to you....Say you believe me."

"I do." She forces a smile through the tears that are dripping down her cheeks.

"But I have done some things that could make you hate me," he whispers, carefully considering his next words. "Things that could destroy everything between us; awful things."

"I could never hate you, Josh," she says, her posture becoming stiff. "I can hate some of the things you do, but I could never hate you as a person. My love for you is too deep and we have a family together. I can't think of anything so bad that it would make me think less of you."

"Oh trust me," he whispers. "There are things."

"Can you let me judge these things for myself?" She touches his knee with her right hand. Squeezing it tenderly, she adds, "Let me decide if I can forgive you. Let me choose if I can live with you after I know your secret, whatever it is."

"Okay, honey," he says, placing his right hand on top of hers and squeezing. "Because I'm tired of keeping secrets from you, I will tell you."

He drains his drink—it goes down hard—and sets down the glass. "Do you know a woman named Rhonda Peterson?"

"No." Lily slowly shakes her head. "I don't think so. Not that I can recall. Who is she?"

"You knew her as Maggie Collins."

He watches as her face goes blank and the colour quickly disappears from her complexion. He knew the name would shock her.

"You mean *the* Maggie Collins?" Her voice is almost a whisper.

"Yes," he nods. "*The* Maggie Collins. She's the woman I've been visiting all these years."

Lily pulls her hand away. Josh can see she is struggling to process what she has just heard. *Too late to put the Genie back in the bottle. We can never go back to where we were just seconds earlier.*

"What?" she asks feebly. "Why? I don't understand."

"I know it's difficult to digest something like this, but please understand. Rhonda—Maggie—is family and I couldn't just abandon her."

"Family? How?" Her head is spinning. "I thought she was a stranger when she came to town, that she didn't know anyone and that she hardly had any contact with you while she was here."

"That was all part of the plan to deflect attention from me," Josh says. "Maggie Collins is my half-sister, sort of, and in fact, I'm also her uncle. I know it sounds twisted, but it's the truth...a perverted truth."

"What are you talking about?"

"It's like this," Josh says. "My father, Gerald, was a sadistic, child-molesting pervert. The old bastard got my sister Missy pregnant when she was just a young teenager. No one in the family knew about the baby because Missy staged her own disappearance, ran away and had the baby, a girl: Maggie. My sister kept Maggie a secret for years and only I stumbled across her by accident when I was in university in Halifax. From that point on, we worked on a plan...a plan of revenge that ended with murder."

"Murder? What do you mean?"

"I mean that I helped Maggie plan the murder of my father and brothers."

"Your entire family?" Lily pulls further back from Josh. "How could you do that?"

"They deserved it after what they put my sister through." He pauses and studies her blank face. "I'd like to say I regret what I did, but I really don't."

"But *murder* ...?"

"I know it's a lot to deal with and that's why I didn't want to tell you."

"You've lived with that secret for all these years?"

"I have, and it has been hard keeping it from you."

"I don't know what to say."

"Don't say anything, honey." He pauses to collect his thoughts. "After it was all over, Maggie fled to Texas and became Rhonda Peterson. I had no contact with her for several years to avoid sus-picion, but after all the smoke had settled we started meeting in different place around the country. I felt I owed it to my sister to maintain contact with Maggie, and I've been sending money to her all these years because we couldn't risk having her go to work. We didn't want anyone to trace her back here to Liverpool. Besides, I figured the old man owed her that much. Like I said, I don't regret anything I did. They deserved everything they got."

"My God." He can see the news has left her stunned. "I had no idea."

"I'm sure you didn't, and that was the plan."

"Wow. It's all been a lie."

"That's the reason I don't care much for Cliff Graham," Josh says. "He's been relentless about this case, and if he has even the slightest inkling I was involved with Maggie, well, it would be game over for me...for all of us. He's always suspected there was more to Maggie's story. I'm the missing link that keeps nagging at him. I'm telling you because I'm tired of what this secret has been doing to us."

"God. I really don't know what to say."

"I told you sometimes the truth is a hard pill to swallow."

"This is the secret you've been carrying around all these years?"

"That's it. Now, the question is, where do we go from here?"

"I don't know. I really don't know."

"Do you still love me? Can you tell me that much?"

"I don't know. I have a lot of thinking to do."

"I'm the same person I was five minutes ago. I'm the person who loves you with everything that I am. I kept the secret because I wanted to spare you from the truth; I was trying to protect you and the kids. Can you understand?"

"I don't know, Josh."

"Do you want me to leave the house? Would that be easier for you?"

"No, the kids wouldn't understand if you weren't here in the morning. But I think you should sleep in another room tonight."

"If that's your wish. I understand."

"It is. And please promise me one thing." She stands up slowly and walks toward the door as if in a trance.

"Anything."

"Before you go to bed, please set the alarms down here."

"I will."

"Please don't forget."

"I won't. I will make sure that's the last thing I do. I love you, Lily. If there is one thing you can be sure of, it's that I love you with all that I am."

She leaves the room without answering him.

"I love you," he whispers, as she closes the door behind her.

He knows she's gone. The question remains, how far has she gone?

Suddenly angry with himself for telling her, he hurls the crystal Scotch glass at the fireplace and watches it shatter into hundreds of pieces.

God damn it. What have I done?

24: Nothing is ever cut and dried

Lily knew Josh had secrets, but she had had no idea they were this serious. What he had told her could change her entire world, but she knows whatever she does with the information could also change the lives of her children. And that's where this all gets foggy for her. She knows, no matter what she does, she must always protect her children. Their well-being must be her first priority, now and forever.

Growing up in Liverpool, she had heard the stories of the Goodwin family, about all the dirty tricks, the scheming, the backstabbing, the womanizing, the backroom politics and underhanded deals that made them the most powerful and feared people in this town. When, as an adult she ended up working for one of them, she concluded most of what she had heard about them was, in fact, true.

Even so, she has always thought Josh was different than the other Goodwin men. She believed that somehow he had managed to climb out of the muck and found his road to success through hard work and determination, and by keeping above the fray. Now, though, she can see it was all lies. Their life together has been built on a foundation of deceit and deception—all of it deadly.

Tonight, as she rolls in her bed, staring at the ceiling, she knows she has a lot of soul-searching to do. Can she live with Josh after everything he's done? He took part in a murder plot that resulted in the death of four people—all members of his own family.

What if everything he says about them was true? Did his family still deserve to die as they did, even if, according to what she has heard, most of them represented evil incarnate? Did that give Josh and Maggie the right to kill them? Doesn't that make him the same as them...or maybe even worse?

She was raised to believe that two wrongs don't make a right, but she also knows that life isn't always simple. Nothing is ever cut and dried, she understands.

But even if the men in Josh's family were all evil monsters, was there no better way than plotting to kill them? Did they not deserve a shot at redemption? Is there redemption for such evil people?

Maybe, she tells herself, *Josh was right. Maybe an eye for an eye was fair and his family deserved everything they received. Maybe his actions were justified.*

"Shit," she sighs. The king-sized bed feels more empty and cold tonight than it ever has.

She now understands what he meant when he warned her that sometimes the truth is a heavy burden to carry. Now she wishes she hadn't pushed him to tell her what he had been hiding for all those years. She should have been content to let things alone, to let the sleeping dog lie, as her father had always said.

But it's too late now. She stares into the blankness that is the ceiling. It's become a familiar sight of late. She knows she can't un-hear the words he spoke. She can't un-do the past and she can't un-murder his family.

What's done is done. She has many tough decisions to make as a result of the truth being set free.

"He loves the boys. He worships them, as they do him. He's a great father," she whispers in the dark. "I know that for certain."

If she breaks up his family, the children will suffer and she'd hate for them to be stuck in the middle of this. *None of this is their fault.* Then she thinks, *What's that they say about the sins of our fathers coming back to haunt their sons?*

It's not her fault Josh did those things. They weren't a couple when all these terrible things happened. But if she doesn't tell the truth, if she doesn't turn him in to Cliff, is she condoning what he did?

But if I don't turn him in to the police, can I continue to live with him? Can I keep his secrets and pretend like nothing happened? Does that somehow make me an accomplice even though I wasn't directly involved? Does it make me a bad person to know these things and then not do anything about them?

She wonders if knowing what he did changes the man he is. Or is he the same man he was before she knew?

"Fuck. Fuck. Fuck," she whispers. But this time saying the word doesn't make her feel any better. She understands there's no easy answer to this. *Why did I have to push so hard for him to tell me?*

It's still early in the morning and Lily resists the urge to get up. She closes her eyes tight and tries to force herself to fall asleep, even though she's sure she will not rest tonight. She may never rest again.

Then she hears a loud popping sound from downstairs that causes her to jump in the bed.

"Josh!" she screams.

That noise was a gunshot.

Vernon Oickle

Graduation Day Again

25: Anywhere but here

"Jesus Christ." Corporal Cliff Graham pulls into the driveway and studies the large white house with the black trim and window sashes, and the front yard that's in immaculate condition. "Je—sus."

Noting three police cruisers and two ambulances have arrived at the scene before him, he puts his car in park and turns off the ignition. The fact the officers on scene called him away from his daughter's graduation means they need someone with experience to guide the investigation from the outset. His gut tells him this is something major.

At least I was able to watch Carly cross the stage and receive her diploma, he thinks, exhaling forcefully and wishing he was still in the crowded gymnasium. *Anywhere but here.* He has no idea what's waiting for him inside that house, but he knows he isn't ready for whatever it is.

Lily? he thinks, opening the car door, reaching out with his left hand, grabbing the roof and pulling his tall frame out of his police cruiser. *Josh?* he wonders. *And the boys? Are they okay? Where are the boys?*

Two officers are stringing the familiar yellow and black police tape around the perimeter of the property. Cliff knows tragedy has again struck this quaint little town and he shivers despite the warmth of the afternoon sun.

He turns his back to the house, leans into the open door of the cruiser, and loses himself for a moment in the play of sunlight through the thick canopy of deciduous leaves surrounding this property where the community's richest people are known to live. All of this beauty. But what will await when he enters the house?

He turns and slams the car door as a young constable approaches. It's her first month on the job, and he already feels sorry for her.

"Sir." She stops, her lip trembling.

"Thank you for being here, Constable Park." Cliff keeps his voice business-like to focus the young officer. "I'm looking for the incident commander. I want to make sure he's kept things in order."

"He's inside, sir."

"Can you tell me what you know?"

"Not very much yet," she whispers.

"I will need a quick debrief before we can determine what to do next. We understand proper procedure, but sometimes, it's necessary to break with protocol. As you are learning, Constable, each case is different. So until we get some facts we are not making any decisions or jumping to any conclusions."

She nods.

"Walk with me."

There seems to be an ever-growing crowd of emergency personnel congregating in the front yard. "My gut says this is one of those cases where special circumstances may come into play, if only because of whom we are dealing with here and the resulting publicity."

"Agreed."

"Did you see the victims, Constable?"

She nods, her eyes wide.

"Were they alive?"

She doesn't respond.

"Dead?"

At this point Constable Park turns her back to him, bends over and throws up on the lawn.

"The first time is the worst." Cliff speaks softly. "Do you want to stay outside and try and control the lookie-loos?"

"Yes, sir," she replies after regaining her composure. "Sorry about that."

"We've all been there."

He turns back to the house, offering up a silent prayer. *Please let the kids be okay.*

A senior constable, Brandon Lantz, is standing guard near the front door. Cliff raises his hand in greeting as he takes the steps to the veranda two at a time. "What's going on here?"

"Sir," the constable's body becomes visibly stiff and rigid. Cliff notes his pale face and the beads of sweat on his forehead. "Am I glad to see you, Corporal."

"I wish I could say I was glad to be here. Give me the rundown."

"Three dead, sir. From what we can tell, it happened within the residence."

"It's a mess in there," the officer finally says. "Blood everywhere."

"Murder? Suicide? Home invasion?"

"Can't tell, sir," the officer answers quickly. "Too soon and too much mess."

"No." Cliff notices a red smudge that could be blood on the dark oak wood of the front door. "Can you tell me when the call came in?"

"9-1-1 got the call just over an hour ago. I took the dispatch and responded right away. I knocked and rang the bell. When no one answered, I went around back and gained access through the patio doors in the kitchen. I found a nightmare inside."

"Who called it in?" Cliff asks.

"A woman. Her name is Samantha Henderson-Webster. She told dispatch she had been trying to reach her friend all morning and when she couldn't make contact she got worried. We haven't spoken with her yet. She called on a cell and we're trying to locate her."

"I know where she is," Cliff says. "She's at the high school gymnasium. She's catering the graduation party there this evening." Send a car to the school to inform Samantha about what's happened here. There won't be any stopping the news once word of this gets out. It will spread like wildfire and I don't want her to hear it that way."

"Yes, sir." Lantz nods again. "I'll see it gets done right away."

"Now you are the officer in charge of the scene. I want you to take control and monitor every process. No one gets in unless they are an investigator. I want everything recorded, no matter how insignificant it seems. Even one minor detail could be the final piece of the puzzle we need to tell the whole story."

"Understood."

"We should also canvass this entire neighbourhood. We need to know if anyone heard or saw anything over the past twenty-four hours that might help us piece together a picture of what happened here."

"All ready on it, sir. I've got two constables on it as we speak and I've called for more backup."

"Good. I want this whole area locked down tight. In fact, I want this whole town locked down. Whoever did this might still be around. Let's put cars on the three exits out of town and check every vehicle."

"Yes, sir. But we may not have enough people to do it all."

"I will call in major crimes for backup. We'll also need the dog and ident units on the scene as quickly as possible. I've got a friend at division I want to call in. These types of cases are her specialty."

"We'll take the help, sir."

"You may as well release the paramedics. Their services won't be needed for a while. We'll call them back if we need their help with transport once the ME is done."

"We do have a survivor. So we may need at least one of those ambulances to stick around for a while longer."

"Adult or child?"

"Male child, sir."

"What's his status?"

"Paramedics say he's in shock, but he doesn't appear to be injured, physically at least."

"Where is he?"

"Still inside."

"Away from the carnage, I hope."

"He's in his bedroom with an officer. What should we do about him?"

"Transport him to the hospital right away. We'll have community services give us a hand with this, but he'll need to see a doctor as soon as he gets there. Call ahead to the hospital and tell them what we've got coming their way. Make sure there is an officer with him at all times and have the officer make note of everyone who comes in contact with the child. Also make sure the kid's clothes are collected."

"Very well, sir," Constable Lantz waves to a paramedic who has been standing on the edge of the lawn. "We'll move him out right away."

"Good."

"There is one more thing you should know, sir, before you slip away to make those calls."

"Yes? What else could there be?"

"Well, sir," the officer sucks in a deep breath. "I really don't know how to describe it."

"Just lay it out for me," Cliff says. He has no patience right now.

"Yes, sir. It's just that I've never seen anything like this in my entire life and it's kind of freaked me out, I guess."

"So just tell me what else you've got."

"Okay. At some point, I suggest you have a look at the back yard."

"Another victim?"

"No sir. Dead birds. Hundreds of them, maybe even thousands. And there are all kinds of them. Sparrows. Robins, Starlings. Blue Jays. Big ones. Little ones. All different colours. It's like they just fell from the sky and died when they hit the ground, all at once, but only in this backyard."

"Any crows among them?"

"I don't know for sure, sir, but now that you mention it, I don't think there are any dead crows. At least I don't remember seeing any. Why do you ask?"

"Just curious. I've seen this sort of thing happen before."

"Seriously, sir?"

"A few times. It's a sign."

"A sign, sir?" the constable looks puzzled. "I don't understand."

"It's an omen, Constable Lantz," Cliff says. "A sign of the tragedy that has just hit this place."

"When you consider what's waiting for you inside, I'd say the birds got it right," the officer says.

26: What the hell happened?

"They're all dead, Kate." Sam sobs into the phone. "I can't believe they're all dead. Can you come home right away? I need you here."

Sounding tinny and distant on her phone in Toronto, where she was on business for her law firm, Kate says, "Calm down, Sam. Please tell me what's going on and who is dead. Take a deep breath honey, and talk to me."

"Can you come home?" Sam asks again between sobs. "I don't want to be alone."

"I've got an important meeting tomorrow morning, but I can cancel it and be home before lunch if you really want me to," Kate says, trying to remain calm.

"Please come home, Kate."

"Okay. I will. Now, tell me what's happened."

"It's terrible. I know things have happened in this town in the past, but even this...Someone murdered them last night."

"Murdered *who*?"

"Lily. Josh. Carter, that poor little boy," Sam sobs. "They're all dead."

"Oh my God," Kate whispers. "What about Alex?"

"He's shook up pretty bad, but he doesn't seem to be hurt physically," Sam says, trying to snuff back her tears so Kate can understand her. "They're keeping him in the hospital for observation. Your brother has been seeing him and I've been there. They cancelled the graduation reception for tonight, which gave me the chance to be with Alex, but I've also got Hunter to take care of. Rebecca is coming to stay with Hunter after she finishes her shift and I'm going back to be with Alex. Thank God your brother found her. She's such a sweetheart."

"But what the hell happened?" Kate probes.

"I don't know. The police are investigating and Cliff is coming to talk to me in the morning about what I know, but I don't know anything. I don't know what happened at Lily's house."

Kate speaks softly. "They aren't accusing you of anything, are they?"

"God no," Sam weeps. "But I'm the one who called 9-1-1. After I couldn't reach Lily, I called the police...and...and Cliff says he needs to talk to me. He's hoping I might know something that could help their investigation."

"Do you?"

"I don't think so. Except Lily was terrified over the past few days because she thought someone was stalking the house. But she already told Cliff about it and he was looking into it. I don't know anything else. What should I do, Kate?"

"You can talk to Cliff," Kate says. "We can trust him. You should cooperate as much as possible."

"I knew Lily was scared," Sam says. "I wanted her to come and stay with me until the police had chance to look into what was going on, but she wouldn't even consider it."

"Did she say why she thought someone would be stalking her?"

"No. I don't think she had any idea."

"This is a terrible tragedy," Kate says. "Does Hunter know what happened? He and Carter were pretty close."

Sam starts crying again. "I had to tell him before he heard it from someone else. I just told him Carter had died. I didn't have any choice but I didn't get into gory details."

"Of course you didn't," Kate says. "How did he take it?"

"Not well, which is another reason I need you to come home."

"I'm looking up phone numbers for the airlines as we speak. I'll be home as quickly as I can. I promise," Kate says. "There's going to be a lot of fallout from this and someone has to watch out for Alex. That kid's whole world has just been turned upside down."

"I know. You drew up Lily's will and you know what her wishes were, so that's another reason why you should come home right away. There's going to be a lot of people trying to stick their noses into things where they don't belong. We've got to make sure Lily's wishes for Alex are honoured. I promised her I would make sure he is taken care of."

"We will. But this won't be easy. Even though the terms of her will spell out very clearly what is to happen with Alex, there will be challenges. That little boy stands to inherit a great deal of money. He's going to be worth millions, and there's going to be a lot of people aching to get their hands on it."

"I can't stand this, Kate," Sam sobs. "Why would something like this happen here? Lily was such a kind and loving person. She would do anything for you, even a total stranger. Why would anyone want to hurt her?"

"You never know what some people are capable of," Kate says.

"That is exactly what I told Lily, but she wouldn't listen to me. Why wouldn't she listen, Kate? If she had come to stay with me, they might all still be alive right now."

"Take a deep breath," Kate says, speaking softly She waits until the sobbing stops. "Now, can you tell me when all of this happened?"

"They found the bodies after I called 9-1-1," Sam says. "I've heard everything you can imagine, from it being a botched robbery, to Josh losing his mind and killing his family before committing suicide."

"Is that possible?"

"I didn't think so, but I suppose anything is possible." Sam sighs heavily. "Stranger things have happened around here."

"I know the police won't rule anything out. But, is it possible something was going on with Josh that would cause him to do such a thing? Was he having business troubles? Were he and Lily fighting? Was he having an affair? Was *she* having an affair?"

"God, Kate. No. Lily wouldn't do anything like that. But I do know she was getting fed up with some of the secrets Josh was keeping."

"What kind of secrets?"

"I don't know, but Lily would become really upset when he would disappear a couples times a year on some kind of mystery business trips. She said she was going to give a Josh an ultimatum —tell her what has been going on or they would be done."

"Maybe that has something to do with what happened. Is it possible this was the result of a business deal gone bad? Maybe he was involved with something illegal. Drugs, maybe?"

"I don't know, and I honestly don't think Lily knew. That's really not the vibe I was getting from her. My problem is, how much do I tell Cliff? What if it has nothing to do with what's happened? Is it really any of his business?"

"You have to tell him about it. He needs to know everything so he can try to get a clear picture of what may have been going on in the house. There might be a connection to his trips. You have to let Cliff decide if there is something to it."

"But it seems like I'd be betraying Lily by telling the police such personal things."

"You can't look at it that way, Sam. You're helping the police find who killed her. This has gone beyond betraying a friendship."

"Should I try to put Cliff off until you can be here when he talks to me?"

"That's a good idea. As a matter of fact, I will call Cliff and talk to him."

"Can you do that?"

"I can and I will. Are you and Hunter going to be okay until I get home? I'm sure Charlie and Rebecca will help as much as they can."

Sam sobs again. "This is so unfair. I can't believe anyone would do this to Lily and that precious little boy. It's so senseless."

"What time is Rebecca going to be there?"

"In about an hour, and then I'm going to the hospital to be with Alex. He must be terrified, the poor little guy. Charlie says he hasn't said a single word since they brought him in. We have no idea what he may have seen or been through in that house."

"Dr. Charlie will take good care of him. If there's one thing I know about my twin brother it's that he's good with children. My immediate worry is who will now come crawling out of the woodwork."

"Well he's got two half-brothers and a half-sister. We know there is no immediate family on Josh's side, but I've always been a little cloudy about Lily's family."

"She does have siblings, doesn't she?"

"Yes, a brother and a sister."

"Do we have to worry about them?"

"I don't know. I know it's strange but for as long as I've known Lily, I never met either of them. It's like they were shipped away when they were kids. I don't ever recall seeing them around here."

"Do you know where they live?"

"I believe the brother lives in Toronto somewhere and I have no idea where the sister is. They weren't very close."

"Do you know why?"

"No. Lily never talked about it. Do you really think one of them would come after Alex?"

"It's always possible when you're talking about large sums of money. I'll start digging around to see what I can find out about them."

"No one can take him from me, can they?"

"No, Lily's will is iron clad, but that doesn't mean someone won't make our lives miserable for a while until things get settled. Some people will do anything when it comes to money."

"Lily wanted him to be with us and that's in there, right?"

"It is. Her will is very clear. She named you his guardian until he's of legal age and you are executor of her will. She left her other children very well taken care of, but the bulk of the estate will go to Alex since he was Josh's only child."

"You're sure?"

"It's all done according to the laws of the land. No one can take Alex from you. It's what his mother wanted and what you agreed to. But ..."

"But what? I don't want to hear any buts."

"It is possible that someone with blood ties could claim they have more right to raise him and we could end up fighting them."

"Lily didn't want her family to raise Alex and I will do everything in my power to make sure it doesn't happen."

"And I will be there to help you. Now, if you're going to be okay, I should really get off the phone and make some calls to see if I can rearrange things and talk with Cliff. I will check back with you in about two hours."

"Okay. I hate to let you go because I feel so alone right now."

"I understand. You've lost a good friend, but you've got to stay strong now for Alex and for Hunter," Kate tells her wife. "I will be home as soon as I can."

"All right," Sam answers. "I love you."

"I love you too. I will talk to you soon."

27: Detective Emily Murphy

RCMP Detective Emily Murphy figures she owes her career projection to her former commanding officer at the Liverpool detachment, where she was posted until two and a half years ago, when she helped him solve a serial murder case in which the killer was targeting young girls. Today, she's assigned to the Major Crimes Unit, based in Halifax, where she works homicide, unsolved murders and missing-persons cases. When she heard the place she formerly called home had been rocked by what appeared to be a triple homicide, she was shocked and immediately contacted her superior officer to request the assignment.

Not again, she thought. *How much bad luck can one place have?*

She wasn't surprised when Corporal Cliff Graham called her, before she could contact him with an offer to help in the case. He told her he felt they could use her skills on this case.

"It's a real mess," he said. "I'm too close to this case to be objective so I need someone with your special abilities."

"Of course," she said.

She understands he wasn't just trying to flatter her. She knows Cliff to be a straight-to-the-point kind of police officer. "I've already started the process to have it cleared with my superiors. If they are okay with it I'll be in Liverpool tomorrow."

With the proper protocol out of the way, she didn't hesitate to hand off her other cases so she could respond to Cliff's request. The Liverpool situation was urgent and required immediate attention.

Besides, she thinks the next morning as she sits across the desk from her former commanding officer and mentor, *I owe him that much*.

"If you don't mind me saying, sir, you look great. You've managed to keep your weight under control and you look one hundred percent."

"Thanks."

"Ha-ha. You haven't changed one bit. I give you a compliment and you blush."

They both laugh when he blushes again.

"Halifax is treating you well?" Cliff's question is more like a statement designed to change the subject. "It looks like the work suits you and I continue to hear really good things about you from the city."

"Yes. It's turned out to be everything I thought it would be. I love the plainclothes work. And having to go undercover sometimes suits me very well." She smiles broadly. "I owe you and Sergeant Paris so much for making this happen for me."

"We didn't do it, detective," Cliff replies. "It was all your hard work and brains that got you there."

"How is he, by the way?"

"Greg, you mean?"

"Yes, sir. Sergeant Paris. Is he well? And his family? How are they doing?"

"I haven't had much contact with him recently. Greg keeps a low profile these days. He's pretty much taken himself off the grid. He won't admit it, but I think he's working his way to retirement in a year or so. He only takes a few select cases a year. The situation with Lucy really took a lot out of him."

"I didn't know him all that well but even I could see it took its toll. He paid a heavy price."

"He's convinced that, if it wasn't for his work, that creep would never have kidnapped her."

"I understand why he would feel that way. I've just recently become engaged to a wonderful man and there isn't a day that goes by when I don't think about him and fear maybe I've put him danger because of what I do."

"Congratulations. He's a lucky man." Cliff says.

"Thank you, sir, but I'm the lucky one. I just hope I don't mess things up."

"I learned a long time ago you can't live your life in fear."

Cliff leans back in the green swivel chair that has moulded to fit him over the years. When he retires at the end of this year, he's already decided he's taking it with him. "It's natural to worry about our loved ones, but, for your own sanity, you have to find a way to put those fears aside and embrace the present moment. Fear can control your life. Don't let it do that to you. The important thing is to always keep your head no matter the circumstances. Never lose focus."

"Good advice, sir. And speaking of sanity, what in God's name happened down here yesterday?"

"I wish I knew." Cliff sighs, pulling forward in the chair again and grimacing. "It's a real mess over at the Goodwin house. Forensics are still working it, but we've pretty much ruled out a murder-suicide scenario. We don't see any signs Josh Goodwin—or Lily, I suppose—was responsible for this. We're pretty close to calling it a triple homicide."

"Do you have any leads? What about suspects? Motives? Are there any clues at all?"

"That's a big *no* to all those questions." Cliff shakes his head. "We're still waiting on the inventory from their insurance company to try and determine exactly what may have been taken, but it wasn't too difficult to tell that whoever did this, also robbed the place."

"Robbery gone bad?"

"That's one possible explanation. Or a robbery staged to cover up the murders."

"Can we go the scene?"

"For sure. The bodies have been removed, but everything else is just as we found it yesterday." Cliff stands up and stretches.

"Well then," Detective Murphy says, rising from her chair. "Let's get over there and get started."

And Then...

28: The mystery of six

"Tell me again where the bodies were found," Detective Emily Murphy says as Cliff parks the police cruiser in the driveway next to the large mansion that's surrounded by yellow and black police tape. It's a stark contrast to the flowering bushes and shrubs that splash rainbows of early-summer colour all over the property.

Studying the façade of the historic structure that has links to other crimes and local mysteries in the past, she notes there is an RCMP constable posted at the front of the house to keep away the curious. She knows there'll be another officer stationed in the backyard for the same reason.

"Much of the carnage was contained in the family room and kitchen areas at the back of the house," Cliff says.

He puts the car's transmission into park and turns off the ignition, then turns to face her. "The forensics guys found traces of blood in the hallway and on the front door, but it's not clear if the blood belongs to one of the victims or the perpetrators, or even if it's human. We are still waiting on DNA to confirm that. But I believe it was from a victim. We know something happened in that area and, when I'm in there, I can't shake the feeling that someone would have tried to get away from whoever was chasing them. But I have nothing to prove it. And there's also blood spatters on the back patio, so something happened out there as well. But the bodies were found in a relatively confined space within the house."

"So, it's likely someone in the family saw their loved ones die. That's hard to think about." Cliff grabs for the door handle with his left hand. "It makes me sick to my stomach when I think about what the bastards did to this family and for God knows what. Money? Vengeance? The thrill?"

Glancing at her, he adds, "Ready to go inside?"

"I am. Let's do this."

"Did you have much contact with these people when you worked here a few years ago?"

"Not really." She shakes her head, her ponytail swaying back and forth. "I knew who they were, obviously, but I never met them."

"Nice people." Cliff fights hard to suppress his emotions. "Lily was especially friendly. I knew her a long time and I liked her very much. No matter where or when you met her she always had a warm smile and a friendly hello. I hope whatever happened here, she and her family didn't suffer much."

"That's the problem when tragedy happens in a small town," the detective says as they reach the bottom of the steps. "When something like this happens, you usually know the people involved."

"Yup. But there are many more positives than negatives about working in a place like this."

"Agreed."

At the top of the steps, Cliff says to the officer posted near the front door. "This is Detective Emily Murphy. She's here to assist with the investigation so she can have free access to the premises anytime she wants it. No one is to get in her way."

"Yes, sir," the young officer replies. "Detective," he says, nodding to Emily.

"Constable." She smiles. "I remember my early days when I did my fair share of guard duty at crime scenes. It's not the most glamorous part of the job, but it's vitally important to keep these scenes locked down so nosy, gossip-seeking people don't contaminate the scene."

"Thank you, ma'am."

"Been here long?" Emily asks.

"Since six this morning," he answers, and she sees a smile creep across his face. She immediately likes the young officer.

"Seen anyone around since you've been here?" Cliff asks.

"Just some curious on-lookers and a few reporters and television crews," the constable answers. "But they all stayed at the bottom of the driveway. Other than that, it's been pretty quiet."

"Quiet's good. We're going to be inside for a while," Cliff adds, pulling on a pair of large white latex gloves. Emily does the same. "If we need you, we'll call."

"Yes, sir," the officer says, acknowledging the subtle order to hold his ground, but to keep his eyes and ears opened.

"Well." Cliff sighs while he opens the heavy oak door to the mansion, pictures of which have now been plastered all over the media and the Internet. "Here we are."

He pushes the door open and he points to the blood smear on the wood. "It looks to me like someone was trying to get out."

They step into the foyer and Cliff closes the door behind them. He points to a pool of blood on the granite tile a few steps from the entrance. "There's more here."

Bending to examine the red stain, Emily says, "I'm thinking maybe they were stabbed. It doesn't look like a spatter from a gunshot."

"That's what I thought, too. And it's clear there was a struggle right here," he says, pointing to a small entrance table that has been pushed aside and a crystal vase lying shattered on the floor. Paintings on the wall are also hanging crookedly. "I'd say someone struggled with the male victim here. I don't think the woman or child would put up this kind of fight."

He points again. "There's a trail of blood leading to and from the family room."

"So, whoever this was, they were already injured by the time they broke for the door," she observes.

"Right."

"Only someone chases after him and reaches him just as the victim gets the door open. He pulls the victim back inside, where they struggle and, in the process, the victim gets stabbed. How did Josh Goodwin die?"

"It was brutal," Cliff says. "The ME says the fatal injury was having his throat cut, but he did have several other injuries consistent with stabbings, and he was shot at least once in the abdomen. We're still waiting on the final autopsy reports."

"The poor guy was tortured," Emily says while following the

blood trail down the foyer. "The trail goes in here."

"Brace yourself," Cliff says. "It's a mess in there."

"Jesus," she sighs as they stand in the archway that separates the hall from the family room.

"Brutal," Cliff says again.

He moves around a large green sofa and toward the centre of the room. "Come this way. I think you'll get a better perspective on things."

She glances around as she follows closely in Cliff's footsteps, being careful to avoid anything that might be evidence. She notes a pile of magazines had been knocked to the floor near the coffee table and she sees vases and glass nick-knacks lie shattered in ruins on the mahogany. Chairs have been knocked over and most of the shelves in the built-in wall unit have been emptied, their contents strewn about the floor. She sees a large blood stain on the sofa. She notes there's blood on the matching armchair and a pool of blood on the floor not far from the chair. "Man," she says. "You weren't kidding."

Cliff nods. "Either someone was looking for something or they wanted us to think this was a robbery gone bad in an attempt to throw us off track."

"Are you thinking this was a hit?"

"I am not ruling anything out and we don't know what Goodwin was involved in. He did have a major fortune, so who's to say he wasn't engaged in something unseemly? Everything is still on the table."

From this position Emily can see into the kitchen and all the way to the patio doors, which she sees have several shattered windowpanes. "A struggle there?"

"Yes. Clearly the point of entry and someone was injured out on the patio. We found blood spatter just outside the doors."

"Someone was jumped there?"

"Most likely Mr. Goodwin," Cliff suggests. "My working theory is he heard something and went outside to check. The alarm company records show someone engaging the security system at twelve-fourteen, which we can presume is when the last person

went to bed for the night. The company then shows the alarms being disengaged at three-fifty-three."

"When all this started?"

Cliff nods. "I think Mr. Goodwin heard something on the patio,
turned off the alarm and went outside to investigate. That's when
all hell broke loose. As for what happened next, it's anyone's
guess."

Emily has many questions bubbling. "How many perps were
there? When did the female victim enter the room? How did the
children end up down here? Why kill them all? In what order did
they die? Does the order tell us anything? Were any of them used
as leverage to force someone to talk?"

"And," Cliff says, "how did the young boy escape? Why wasn't he
harmed?"

"Maybe because of his age?"

"Maybe. We found one other really strange thing."

"I'm almost afraid to ask what that would be."

"We found crow feathers in the room."

"Shit," she reacts. "How in the hell would crow feathers get in
here, and why?"

"Those are both good questions."

"So how many feathers are we talking about? One? Two?"

"We found six black feathers in here," he says. His eyes linger on
the furthest corner from the sofa and chair, where most of the
blood is located. "And they were found over there."

"That's a mystery, isn't it?"

"Nothing is ever simple in this town, detective. So how do you
want to do this?"

"I would like to concentrate on the inside of the house," she says.
"If that's okay with you?"

"It is," Cliff nods. "I'll look around outside. There's something I
want to check out."

29: The third time

Hundreds, Cliff thinks while carefully stepping around the corpses of birds littering the Goodwin backyard, their beaks and thin, stiff legs stretching lifelessly to the sky they once ruled. The sight causes him to shiver despite the warmth of this sunny, late-June morning.

He's seen this happen twice before since being posted in Liverpool. The first time was when a young reporter came to town to investigate the deaths of four members of the Goodwin family which coincided with the arrival of the mysterious Maggie Collins. That file has never been solved to his satisfaction and it remains his one nagging case as his retirement draws near.

He'd like to see the file closed before he ends his policing career, but he fears it's not likely. It's the pretty blonde reporter he remembers now as he recalls the hundreds of crows falling to the pavement in the detachment's parking lot while she was sitting in his office, interviewing him for her story on the Collins girl.

What was her name? he thinks, as he pauses to examine the broken and bloodied remains of two young robins who hit the ground almost in the same spot, their bodies meshed grotesquely together. "Hannah Simms," he finally says to no one. "Yes," he nods as he wipes the sweat from his forehead and continues walking. "It was Hannah Simms."

He remembers that she, too, died in mysterious circumstances, at Haddon House while working on her story. He also remembers the young officer, Mike Cahill, who accidentally killed Hannah when his gun misfired. Then, a year later, he too died, at the hands of a crazed killer on a warped mission of revenge.

"Haddon House," Cliff mutters as he makes a beeline to the stand of trees at the perimeter of the Goodwin estate that provided the property with a buffer zone from the road on the other side. He remembers how opulent Haddon House once was. A world class bed and breakfast that attracted visitors from around the globe. Now it's empty and rotting. *How does that happen? What a damned waste.*

Cliff reflects on the property's glory days, when Viola and Ronald Toole operated the place with pride and care. He knows if they were alive today, they'd be heartbroken to see the state of the property. Today, the historic structure, which is destined to become town property because of back taxes, is deserted and will likely remain so well into the foreseeable future, he thinks, as no one wants to buy a place which was the site of such horrific acts of violence against children. It's there that young Lucy Paris, his best friend's daughter, almost died. And that case had almost destroyed the man he's known since they graduated from depot together, all those years ago.

He's heard rumours that some of the locals want Haddon House demolished, and he's sure in time the once stately structure will fall to the wrecker's ball, although around these parts they don't actually use wrecker's balls to knock down buildings. Instead, they use backhoes and bulldozers to do the work. *Regardless*, he shrugs, *the result is the same—an empty lot.*

Perhaps, he thinks, *they can build a park on the property as a memorial to the young victims who died there, but that's not my call.*

The second time he witnessed the bodies of dead birds on the ground like this was about two years ago, when he and Greg Paris visited the home of Clara Underwood out on Gull Island Road, while investigating the child killer known as Lucas McCarthy.

Now that was weird, Cliff thinks as he reaches the outer tree line and locates the path he had followed the other day.

Birds falling from the sky was bad enough, he thinks. *Then we go inside and find out she had just lain down on her bed and died, hugging her Bible to her chest. Very weird.*

Whenever he thinks of the incident he can't shake the feeling that the old woman knew she was going to die. It was clear she simply closed her eyes and drifted off to whatever places wait on the other side.

I will never get that image out of my head. I've amassed far too many images over the years especially during my time in this town. I wonder if I'll be able to relax in retirement after experiencing all this weirdness. But it's time to find out.

He's looking forward to stepping back from all the excitement and maybe finally enjoying some down time, something he hasn't had a lot of for most of his adult life. He's confident he'll find some-thing to keep himself occupied.

What is it about this town and the crows? Cliff wonders as he trudges through the underbrush and arrives at the clearing he had discovered the other day. He remembers the blood on the leaf and checks to see if it is still there. It is and he reminds himself he should have a forensics unit stop by here and check the place out, something that has been on his to-do list for two days.

It's not like me to put these things off. Too much on my mind, I guess.

Standing in the small clearing, he suddenly feels as though he's being watched. He drops his right hand to the handle of the pistol that fits snuggly against his hip in its leather holster and scans the area, searching for anyone—or anything—that might be observing him.

"Is someone here?" He barks.

His eyes are drawn to a large rock surrounded by a group of birch and maple trees, where he sees the unmistakable form of a child trying to hide.

"Who's there?" He asks again, more softly. "Please come out and show yourself."

"Yes, sir."

A young boy emerges from the underbrush.

"Who are you, son, and what are you doing back here? You're really close to a major crime scene."

The child nods. "Yes, sir," he says, slowly approaching Cliff. "I know. I was just watching."

"What's your name?"

"Dillon Davis." The boy answers, casts his eyes to the ground as if he's been caught doing something naughty. "Is it true that they're all dead?"

"Some, yes." Cliff nods. "Dillon? As in the Dillon who was bullying the young Pittmann boy?"

"I didn't mean anything by it," Dylan whispers, his words barely audible even though it's deathly quiet under the trees. "I just meant to have some fun with him."

"Bullying is not a joke. Did you ever stop to think about how Carter was feeling when you were making fun of him?'

The boy shakes his head. "No, sir." Cliff can see the tears starting to fall. "Is Carter dead?"

"Is that what you've heard?"

He nods.

"Who told you he was dead?"

"My mom. She said he was shot." He pauses and then asks, "Is that true?"

"I can't tell you how anyone died, Dillon," Cliff says. "But yes, I am afraid he's dead."

"Why?" the boy cries.

"I can't discuss any of that, son," Cliff says. "By the way, do you often play in these woods?"

"Yes, sir. Not every day, but I'm here a lot."

"Tell me, Dillon. Have you ever seen anyone else while you were in here?"

"Like who?"

"Any strangers? People you don't know or recognize from around town or maybe even someone you *do* recognize?"

"No, sir Why?"

"Just asking," Cliff says. "I thought you might have seen something that could help us."

"No people," Dillon says. "But I did see the same car around there the past few days and that seemed weird."

"Weird? How?"

"Most of the cars just drive by and keep going wherever they go But this car would slow down and drive back and forth, and I even saw it stopped a few times."

"Can you show me where it was parked?"

"Yes."

The boy turns and sprints through the underbrush, with Cliff following close behind. Reaching the road, he points to the shoulder.

"Here?" It's where Cliff saw tire tracks in the loose gravel when he was here the other day.

"Yes," the boy nods, pointing. "And there, and there."

"How many times did you see this car?"

"I don't know. Five, maybe six times over the past couple of days."

"Did you recognize the car as one you saw around here before?"

"No."

"What colour was it?"

"Light brown."

"Or beige?"

"Maybe," he shrugs, "but it had a lot of rust on it."

"Notice if it was a two door or a four door?"

"Four-door."

"You're sure?"

"Yes," the boy nods again. "Four doors."

"Notice anyone in the car?"

"I couldn't really see into it."

"Notice anything else, Dillon?"

The boy pauses then blurts out, "The licence plate."

Cliff's pulse quickens. "You get the number?"

"No." Dillon shakes his head. "But it was red, white and blue."

"See any of the writing on it?"

"Didn't get a good look because it was covered in mud but it did have a picture of a flower."

Cliff considers this. "You're sure it was a flower?"

The boy nods.

"Thank you for your help, Dillon," Cliff pulls a business card from the left breast pocket of his shirt and passes it to the boy. "Can you please ask your mom or dad to give me a call at the number on this card?"

"Am I in trouble?" the boy asks and Cliff can see his body immediately becoming tense.

"No, you are not in any trouble. Actually, you have very good observational skills. I am impressed. Perhaps you might become a police officer when you grow up."

Cliff pauses, watching the boy's face and waiting for the tiny seed to land. "However, I think you should go on home now and I may want to speak with you again. Will that be okay?"

"Yes," he answers and Cliff see he's on the verge of tears again.

"Something else on your mind?"

As the tears drip from his brown eyes, the boy says, his voice almost a whisper, "I am sorry for what I did. I didn't mean to make Carter feel bad."

"I know," Cliff says gently. "Now go on home and don't forget to give that card to your parents. It's important that I speak to them."

"I won't forget," Dillon says as he turns and checks for traffic before crossing the street.

Cliff watches until he's sure the boy has made it safely across the road, then turns back into the woods.

Red, white and blue. He tries to remember all the colours of the licence plates from provinces and states he's seen around town. He hopes the boy's description can lead them to whomever is responsible for this crime.

He pushes through the underbrush and heads back toward the house, thinking the red, white and blue licence plate with the flower on it could be a clue. *It could also be nothing, but at least I've now got something to chase.*

30: Froot Loops

On the patio, Cliff pauses at the double French doors and considers the shattered windowpanes. Looking at the glass strewn about the tiles and studying the pattern of the pieces still resting where they landed over twenty-four hours earlier, he tries to imagine what happened. It seems someone was either shoved against or stumbled through these doors, breaking the windows in the process.

Noting the drops of blood near the doors and the trail of blood leading through the kitchen, into the family room and then down the hallway to the front foyer, he thinks this is likely where the carnage began. Then it escalated to the family room, where the killings occurred. What horrors these people suffered he can only imagine. What happened here was an extreme act of violence carried out by someone with no remorse.

What could make someone brutalize another person like this?

He studies the blood patterns, considering the size of the drops, the directionality and the shapes of the spatters. He'll admit he's no forensics expert, but he's attended enough crime scenes throughout the years to know the blood spatters can tell a story. If you know how to read them, they can give you valuable evidence.

He scans the room, noting the box of Froot Loops on the kitchen counter. The image causes him to think about the children, one left dead and another left traumatized, possibility emotionally scarred for the rest of his life.

What could push someone to kill a kid? He realizes that, after almost thirty years in policing, there are no easy answers to questions like this.

Some people, he thinks, *are monsters, and that's the bottom line.*

He knows people like that can disconnect from reality. They don't think or act like normal human beings and they have no compassion for anyone else. Least of all, they can't understand the ramifications of their actions.

"Sociopaths," he whispers.

He stops at the kitchen island and glances toward the family room, seeing Emily crouched near the over-sized green armchair with a large bloodstain soaked into the plush material. She's studying the spatters, which have now turned a morbid shade of near black. He knows this is where Lily Pittmann was sitting when she died, so whatever she saw, it was from this position. That is the vantage point Emily is trying to duplicate.

"Find anything?" he asks as he enters the shattered room.

"These people were put through hell," she says. "This whole thing makes me really sick."

"I'm with you there," Cliff says. He stays put and lets the detective do her work.

"There's a lot of anger and rage evident. This place was trashed big time." Emily stands and glances at the blood-soaked sofa across from her, where Josh Goodwin must have died. "But the one thing that really bothers me is the location of the little boy who survived."

"I don't follow." Cliff looks puzzled. "I'm guessing there was a lot of confusion when everything went down and the boy just scampered to the corner to get away from whoever was killing his family. Maybe it's as simple as he was running for cover and somehow managed to survive, by the Grace of God."

"By the grace of something," she says. "But I don't think it's as simple as that."

"What do you mean?"

She moves to a corner of the room. "The constable found Alex Goodwin hunkered down right here. That doesn't feel right to me."

Glancing back toward the centre of the room, she adds, "They had a clear shot of the boy, so why didn't they take him out? If, they were eliminating potential witnesses, why did they leave him alive? Clearly, from here, he could see everything that happened.

There's no doubt he knows who did this."

"Maybe because of his age they couldn't bring themselves to harm him," Cliff suggests. "Maybe they thought he wouldn't be able to tell us anything."

"I'm not sure I buy that, either," she says. She looks at the corner more closely. "They didn't hesitate to kill the other child and he was only a few years older, so what was so special about this one? I think if the killings were about protecting their skins, they would have taken out the boy. But maybe something happened that prevented them from doing it."

"Who knows how these kind of people think? Maybe they were interrupted. Maybe they ran out of time. Maybe something scared them off. Whatever happened, I'm glad they didn't harm him."

"So am I, but here's another thing," Emily says, flipping through the file she brought with her from the detachment. "It says in these reports that six crow feathers were found near this corner. What's a crow doing in here when three people are being massacred? And why in the hell were the feathers only here and not anywhere else in the room?"

"Let me warn you right now, detective," Cliff says, his posture becoming stiff and his head spinning as it does whenever talk turns to weird crow behaviour. "Don't go trying to figure out those freaking black birds, or it will drive you nuts. I've been there and it's not a place you want to go. Trust me, when you start talking about the crows around here, you're heading to a dark place."

"Seriously?" She looks at him, puzzled. "You don't think it's strange we found crow feathers in our crime scene?"

"I absolutely do." He nods and wipes the sweat from his forehead. He suddenly finds it very hot and stuffy in the room. "It's strange, make no mistake about that, but if you're looking for easy answers with anything connected to those bloody crows, you won't find them. I've chased these birds for a long time and I have always come up empty-handed. Whatever secrets they have, they keep them well protected."

"This doesn't sit well with me," Emily says. "There's something going on here that does not add up."

"And maybe it never will," Cliff says. "I'm not trying to discourage you, but nothing ever adds up when the crows are involved."

He sees she doesn't know how to respond to his comment. "Anything else, detective?"

"Well, I think there were three intruders."

"What makes you think so?"

"The position of the bodies, for one thing, and the amount of damage," she says. "It just seems like too much for one or two people. And I believe this was personal."

"Why?" His eyebrows now rise in curiosity.

"The position of the victims." She pulls photos from the file. "See here. They moved the family into a circle so they could see each other. Intruders on a rampage who were randomly killing people wouldn't do that. They wouldn't care where these people died. The killers wanted the family members to see each other's fear and suffering. They wanted them to see each other die. That's a personal statement."

"It is a good point," Cliff says. "This does feel personal."

"They were torturing them and making the others watch."

"The question is, why?"

"Control. Payback. Trying to make someone talk," she suggests. "Who really knows? So now what? Did you find anything out back that might help?"

"I may have actually found us a lead."

"And that would be?"

"A possible licence plate. Not a number." Cliff glances at his watch. "A boy who knew these kids gave me a description of a car and the plate. It's a good starting point and we can pursue it once we get back to the detachment. For now, though, we have to go and talk with Alex. Kate Webster wanted us to wait until she got back from Toronto. She was due home by now, so we should be going to meet with them—that is, if you are done here. I don't want to rush you."

"I am done for now but I will want to come back later."

"Come back whenever you want," Cliff says. "I don't want to interrupt you if you're onto something, but I do want you to talk to the kid. I understand that connecting with young witnesses has really become your specialty and it's one of the reasons I called you in to assist with the investigation. I knew we were going to have to speak with the boy and I wanted someone I could trust."

"I'm getting a reputation?" she says, following Cliff from the family room and into the foyer.

"Just be happy it's a reputation for something good."

"I guess," she chuckles, then glances back at the blood-soaked room. "But talking to children connected to these types of crimes is the hardest part of the job."

31: It was black

"Corporal," Kate Webster says as she opens the front door to the quaint bungalow she shares with her wife, Samantha Henderson, and their adopted son, seven-year-old Hunter. Extending her right hand and smiling warmly she adds, "Nice to see you again, but why is it that we always seem to meet under such horrendous circumstances?"

"It's the nature of our work, I think." Cliff smiles back and grasps her hand. "Sorry we're late. We got bogged down."

"Come in," she says to the pair of police officers. "It's okay. I was running a little behind myself this morning. The plane was about fifteen minutes late getting in to Halifax and then there was a lot of traffic coming from the airport." She shakes her head. "I can't get over how many crazy drivers there are on the road at such an early hour. I swear some of them must have a death wish."

"Trust me," Cliff says, stepping into the entrance hallway with Emily, "there are crazy drivers on the road no matter what time of day you're talking about. I'm surprised there aren't more people killed."

Kate turns to the young woman in street clothes. "Hi. I'm Kate Webster. I don't believe we've met."

"I'm Detective Emily Murphy. You may not remember me, but we met several times when I was posted here."

"I thought you looked familiar. I apologize. You look different. Must be the hair. I'm usually much better at remembering people, but I am a little distracted this morning."

"Perfectly understandable, Ms. Webster." Emily smiles warmly. "I'm sure you've got a lot on your mind."

"Please don't call me Ms. Webster in my own house. I get enough of that in the office and courtrooms. It's Kate."

"Okay." Emily nods. "Kate it is." Then the detective adds, "I guess you know why we're here?"

"I do." Kate turns and starts down a bright yellow hallway with dark-brown tiles. "Come this way, please. Alex is in the living room with Sam."

"How is he?" Cliff asks as he and Emily follow closely behind.

"He hasn't said a single word since Sam brought him home from the hospital last night."

"That's understandable," Emily says. "He's witnessed a tremendous trauma and his mind is trying to protect him."

"I appreciate you have to speak with him, but I'm not sure how he can help you if he can't or won't talk."

"Maybe talking to someone different may encourage him to open up," Cliff suggests. "We have to try."

"Of course you do." Kate pauses. "Charlie...that's my brother. He's a doctor. He says not to push him to get him to try to speak. He needs to do this on his own. Charlie says forcing him may only make him retreat even further."

"I promise you," Emily says, "we will take it easy. We are not here to harm him. We'll just talk to him and see if he talks back to us. If not, we'll try something else. We are also concerned for his well-being."

"Of course," Kate replies, continuing down the hallway until she reaches the living room door. "They're in here."

"Thanks, Kate," Cliff says. He takes her hands and squeezes them gently. "I promise you we'll be easy on him. By the way, how is your son doing with all of this?"

"He's not doing so well." Kate sighs. "He and Carter were pretty close so he's very upset. He's with Charlie and Rebecca this morning so he won't be here for this, but he doesn't understand what's happened to his friend."

"None of us do," Cliff admits.

He and Emily step into the warmly-decorated living room that looks like something he's seen on one of those television home makeover shows his daughter likes to watch and that he endures for the sake of her company.

After greeting Sam and making introductions, Cliff turns to the small boy sitting close to Samantha, her arm wrapped tightly around him. He kneels in front of the boy. "Hi, Alex. I don't know if you remember me. My name is Cliff and I was a friend of your mom and dad."

The boy says nothing. He doesn't blink. He remains still and stares at the living room wall where a seascape is hanging. Cliff recognizes Summerville Beach and remembers the times he and his children spent there when they were younger and visited him each summer, but he quickly shakes the images from his head. He knows he can't be distracted.

"I understand you're sad, Alex," he says, keeping his voice low and mellow. "We are all very sad for what has happened."

The boy remains silent and still. Cliff wonders if he's even hearing what he's saying.

"Is it okay if my friend here talks to you for a few minutes? Her name is Emily and I think you'll like her very much."

There is no response.

"I am going to let Emily talk to you now but at any time if you want her to stop, you just let us know and we'll stop. If you don't feel like talking, that's okay, too."

Cliff stands and makes way for the detective as she moves closer to the sofa.

"Hi Alex," Emily says, smiling warmly. "May I sit beside you right here on the sofa?" He doesn't respond, and after a moment she sits next to him. She glances at Sam, waiting for her to give the go-ahead. Seeing the nod, she proceeds.

"Alex, I know this is really, really hard and, like Cliff said, whenever you want to stop you just let me know. Is that okay?"

He stares blankly past her.

"Alex," she says. "Do you remember the night when the people came to your house?"

He says nothing.

"Were you sleeping when they came?"

He says nothing.

She waits a few moments as silence fills the room. "Did you hear them and then come downstairs?"

The boy does not respond.

"Did you see who hurt your mommy and daddy and your brother?"

She pauses, looks at Sam then turns back to Alex. "Did you see who hurt Carter?"

He continues to stare at the ocean scene.

Emily decides to change tactics. "Do you like the ocean, Alex?"

It's not much, but she sees him nod slightly.

"I like the ocean, too. I like the feel of the warm sand between my toes and looking for seashells, especially sand dollars. I really like jumping in the waves. Do you?"

She can just barely see the movement, but she's sure he nodded.

"When I was your age, me and my family used to go the beach every weekend in the summer," Emily tells him, keeping her voice soft and gentle. "We'd stay for the whole day and I loved it. My sister and I liked to build castles in the sand and then watch as the waves would come and wash them all away. Did you and Carter like to be build sandcastles?"

She waits to see if the boy responds. He doesn't.

Pushing on, she says, "We'd always take a picnic with us. My mom would spread a blanket on the sand and put all the food out and we would eat it all right there on the beach. It was a lot of fun. Did you ever have a picnic on the beach with your family, Alex?"

He doesn't respond.

"This isn't working," Kate whispers to Cliff. The two of them have been standing back by the door, watching.

"Give her a little more time," Cliff urges. He knows these things can take a while, but he hopes the detective can get through to the boy because, without him, they may have a difficult time breaking this case. He knows an eyewitness would speed things up immensely. "Just a few more minutes."

"I noticed you had a nice big pool at your house," Emily continues. "Do you like swimming and playing in the pool, Alex?"

There is no response.

"I've been to your house, Alex," she continues, knowing that repeating his name as often as possible may encourage him to see her as a friend. "You have a beautiful home. Did you like it there? I bet you had lots of fun playing there in the backyard."

He continues to remain quiet and still.

"You are very sad, aren't you, Alex?" she whispers. "I understand why you are sad….Can you talk to me about why you're sad?"

He remains quiet.

"It's okay to be sad," she says. "When my sister died, I was sad for a very long time and I'm still sad about it. I miss her every day, but I keep her with me in my memories and in my dreams. You'll be able to do that with your mom and dad and brother."

She pauses and waits to see if he responds, but he says nothing. However, she notes a tear trickle down his tiny cheek.

"You can cry, Alex," she whispers. She can see Sam is becoming concerned about the boy's emotional status and Emily knows she's running out of time. "I still cry about my sister."

Tears are flowing now.

"Is there anything you remember about that night you can tell us, Alex?" she gently probes. "No matter what. Anything that comes to your mind."

Seconds later, Sam speaks up, "I'm sorry, detective, but I really think that's enough for now. He really should rest."

"Yes, for sure," Emily nods. "It's fine. I understand." She turns to Cliff and Kate and shakes her head.

"All right then," Cliff says. "I guess it is time for us to be going. Thanks for seeing us, Alex. It was really nice to see you again, but we're going now. If you think of anything you want to say to us, you tell Sam and Kate and they can call us right away."

To Emily, Cliff asks, "Are you ready to pursue that other lead?"

"Yes," she says, beginning to rise from the sofa.

As she slowly rises, Alex reaches out with his right hand and grabs her left hand. Caressing the modest diamond engagement ring on her slender finger he whispers, "Ring."

Emily keeps her hand in position. "Ring? What ring Alex?"

"Ring," he whispers again.

"Who has a ring?" she asks, as the others in the room remain quiet. "Did your mom have a ring, Alex?"

Silence reigns over the room for several seconds as the adults exchange glances. Finally, the boy says, "The woman had a ring."

"What was the ring like Alex?" Emily asks. "Can you describe it for me?"

"It was black," he whispers as the tears continue to flow down his cheeks. "The ring was black."

32: A theory, at least

"Sorry to keep you waiting," Sam says, "but thanks for sticking around long enough for me to put Alex down for a nap."

They are in the living room, where Kate has been talking with the two RCMP officers.

"He didn't get much sleep last night, as I'm sure you can appreciate, so he was pretty tired. I think he fell asleep as soon as his head hit the pillow. I'm just sick for him."

"It's no trouble. Poor little guy," Cliff says, smiling at the woman he met on the first day he came to Liverpool, more than twenty years ago. Back then she was running Henderson's, the family's general store. It was a great place, he remembers, but she had to close it down about five years ago, when competition from the big box stores and rising costs became too much for her handle.

Now she runs a highly-successful catering business and there has been talk around town she may run for mayor in the next elections, but she hasn't confirmed that to anyone. Cliff believes that, if she did run for office, she'd get elected. He knows he'd be hard-pressed to find anyone in this town who doesn't like Samantha Henderson. He's sure he would vote for her.

"We're only too glad to stick around and talk, if it might lead to something that could help us," he adds. "The sooner we find whoever did this, the better it will be for the entire town. Everyone's on edge and jumping at their own shadow."

Emily says to Sam, "If you don't mind me saying, you are very good with him."

"He's a special little boy," Sam replies, as Kate takes her left hand and squeezes it gently. "Lily was my friend, so I've gotten to know him very well. I spent a lot of time with him over the years, so I guess he's used to me being around."

"I think it's more than that," Emily says. "It's easy to see there's a special bond between the two of you."

"Did I hear right yesterday," Cliff asks, "that you will be his legal guardian?"

"That's right," Kate quickly answers, her instincts as a lawyer kicking in. "Lily appointed Sam as Alex's legal guardian in her will. She took care of all the paperwork about a year ago, and it's a good thing she did. You just never know when tragedy will hit."

"You never know," Sam whispers, shaking her head and fighting hard to hold back the tears that threaten to break through the dam.

"I think Lily made a great choice," Cliff says. "Alex is going to need a lot of support and it's important he be with people who will look out for his best interests."

"Yes," Sam sighs. "Lily knew Kate and I would love him and take care of him as if he were our own son."

"He is," Kate jumps in. "Once the will goes through probate and the paperwork is processed, for all intents and purposes you will be his mother, as far as the law is concerned."

"You'll do fine." Cliff smiles at Sam. "You're already a wonderful mother. You both are. Hunter is a great little boy."

"We try, but there are times," Sam says.

"I know what you mean," Cliff says. "My kids are grown up now, but I remember what they were like when they were young. They all have their moments."

"Now," Sam says, "let's talk about what Alex said. I was thinking about that while I was helping him get into bed."

"Do you have any idea what he was talking about?" Emily asks. "Did his mother have a black ring he could be recalling?"

"No." Sam slowly shakes her head. "Not that I ever saw, anyway. However, and I'm not sure if this is important, I do remember once, when Lily and I were talking about our favourite pieces of jewellery and family heirlooms, she told me about a beautiful black onyx ring her own mother once had, and how much she admired it."

"Might be nothing," Cliff agrees. "But you never know. Any idea where that ring might be now?"

"I have never seen it personally, so I have no idea," Sam says. "But I do remember Lily telling me her mother gave the ring to her granddaughter, Gwen. That's Lily's daughter, and Lily told me she could never understand why her mother would give such a valuable item to her, as Gwen was always in so much trouble. She feared Gwen would lose the ring or sell it."

"So, the ring belonged to Gwen's grandmother?" Emily asks.

"Yes," Sam nods. "But, like I said, it's probably nothing. And God knows what Gwen would have done with it. She probably sold the ring to get money to buy drugs. She was a handful, that one. She gave Lily so many headaches."

"Just for argument's sake," Cliff says, "do you have any idea where Gwen is these days? I haven't seen her around here in a few years, but I remember she gave Lily a great deal of grief when she was growing up. We never charged her with anything that I can recall, but we had a few close run-ins with her and I always wondered how she had gotten so far off track. Lily was good to her and the other Pittmann kids turned out to be nice young gentlemen."

"I'm really not sure where she is," Sam says. "She and Lily didn't get along very well and in the last year or so Gwen stopped calling her. I think the last time she called was four or five months ago and that ended in an argument, according to what Lily told me."

"You mean she didn't call to check on her son?"

"Not very often. And I can tell that really upset Lily."

"I'm sure it did," Cliff says. "I would be upset, too. Do you know what they argued about?"

"Not that time. But if it was like other times in the past, it was probably about money. Gwen was always asking her mother for handouts and, although Lily didn't know for sure, she suspected Josh was sending her money as well."

"Can you remember the last time when Gwen called, where she was living? Did Lily ever say anything about that?"

"I'm pretty sure she was somewhere in Alberta," Sam says. "That was a while ago, so God only knows where she is now."

Cliff turns to Emily. "What colour are the license plates in Alberta?"

"I'm not one hundred percent certain," the detective answers. "But I think they've got a white background and I'm pretty sure there's some red and blue on them."

"That's what I thought." Cliff pauses and then asks, "Do they have a flower on them?"

"Now you're really testing me." Emily pulls her phone out of her jacket pocket. "But just give me a minute and I'll check."

A few seconds later she nods. "They've recently changed them, but the older plates in Alberta feature the wild rose. It's the provincial flower."

"Is that so?" Cliff frowns.

Emily turns the phone for him to see. "It says so right here. Why?"

"Remember back at the Goodwin house when I told you I might have found a lead?" Cliff says.

She nods.

"When I was out looking around in the woods that separate the Goodwin property from Elm Street, I ran into a kid who told me he had seen a light brown—maybe beige—car hanging around there recently. Guess what he told me about the car's license plate?"

"That it was white, red and blue?" Emily answers. "And let me guess again: He said it had a picture of flower on it."

"Bingo. He didn't know the number because it was covered in mud."

"Cliff," Kate interrupts the officers. "Do you think Gwen Pittmann came back to town and killed her own son and mother?"

"And Josh?" Sam adds.

Cliff realizes he should not have been revealing case details like that, even to women he trusts. It's not like him to make such a slip-up. "I don't want to jump to any conclusions until we get some proof. But this ring Alex saw could be another clue that points to her. If not her, then maybe someone who was with her, but I bet she was there. It's a theory at least and so, far it's the only thing we have."

"Why?" Sam cries as Kate slips her right arm around her wife and hugs her tightly. "Why would she do that to her own child and her own mother?"

"I have no idea. And I'm not saying it was her," Cliff says. He pulls himself out of the large chair. "But if we find her, we'll be able to ask her."

"Where to, corporal?" Emily asks as she also stands.

"For now, back to the detachment," Cliff says. To Kate and Sam, he says, "Perhaps you could keep to yourselves what we have just been talking about. It's only a theory, and I don't want to worry people."

Sam nods. "We're not talking about any of this mess to anybody."

"Absolutely, Cliff," Kate says. "We want to do whatever we can do to help."

"I appreciate that."

When they have left the house, Cliff says to Emily, "I want a North America-wide bulletin issued for that car. And if it's any-where in Nova Scotia I want it found as quickly as possible. Let's hope they haven't left the province already. After we set that up, let's head back to the house. Now that we have an idea who might be responsible for this, maybe we'll see things differently."

33: Aren't you tired of this?

"I can't believe it took less than three hours for someone to spot the vehicle," Emily says as she and Cliff head down the hall to the cubical-like detention room where Gwen Pittmann is being held for questioning. "Why in the hell didn't they high-tail it out of the province, put some distance between them and this town?"

"People get careless and they panic, especially when they're on the run."

"I know, but parking right out in the open for everyone to see?" Emily shrugs. "That's not careless, that's just plain stupid."

He remembers that the car was in the parking lot of a Bridgewater motel. "They didn't even try to conceal themselves."

Quickly scanning the arrest report as they near the room, Cliff notes that, although there was some resistance, the woman and two men were apprehended at the scene without incident. They were brought back to the Liverpool detachment.

Cliff sighs deeply, his chest tightening as he opens the heavy steel door and they enter the small room. Its air is so ripe with body odours, he wants to vomit on the cement floor. He studies the scrawny, dishevelled woman in oversized, dirty clothes that hang loosely on her body. To him, she looks like she just crawled out of bed and hasn't had a shower in a week or a good meal in a month.

Hard-looking ticket, he thinks, as he approaches the small wooden table in the middle of the room. He pulls out a wooden chair and sits. The detective pulls out a second chair and sits beside him, directly across from the suspect.

Gwen jumps as Cliff slams a ruled notepad on the table. He watched this woman grow up as a precocious child and turn into a troubled teenager who gave her mother nothing but grief and heartache, despite the fact Lily was one of the most caring and thoughtful women he had ever known. Now, he feels nothing but disgust for Gwen because he's confident that if she didn't do it personally, then she knows which of the two men she was travelling with were responsible for the torture and execution of her family.

If it were up to him, he'd lock up all three of them and throw away the key. But it's not up to him. He's just the grunt out on the streets rounding up this scum and, as a law enforcement officer, he knows there are lines he can't cross. Recalling some of the criminals who have received light sentences over the years for serious crimes, he just wishes the courts would also see it his way.

Cliff opens the notepad and stares at the young woman. He sees drooping eyes, a dazed expression, pale complexion and an emaciated body. He asks, "Cocaine? Heroin? Crack? What were you on?"

Gwen looks at him, her eyes half closed and her eyeballs sunken into their sockets, but she says nothing. He can sense her disdain for him.

Emily says, "Look, Gwen, you may as well talk to us and tell us what happened at the house. We've got you and, with or without your cooperation, the three of you are going away for a very long time. The question is, do you want to go away with three first-degree murder charges on your record or do you want to go away on a lesser charge and maybe spend less time behind prison bars? It's totally your call."

"Because," Cliff jumps in, "make no mistake about it, young lady, you are going to jail."

"Don't I get a lawyer?" the young, woman asks. The tattoos on her neck and arms do nothing to impress the police officers. "I ain't saying nothin' until I get a lawyer."

"You can wait for a lawyer," Gwen says. "If you don't have one Legal Aid can provide one. But they are awfully busy these days, so you may be sitting here a very long time until someone shows up. Or you can make this easier on yourself and talk to us right now. It's your choice, but if I was in your shoes, I'd be doing everything in my power to make this easier on myself."

Cliff knows he should keep his mouth shut, but he jumps in.

"What were you thinking?" He slaps the table with the palm of his right hand. "What in the hell were you thinking when you watched your family being slaughtered? Your own son, for God sake? Your own mother. Jesus! I guess you weren't thinking, were you? So, Gwen, I'm asking again, what are you on?"

The woman tries to pull herself into a seating position but doesn't have the strength to sit up straight. She shrugs.

"Listen to me," Emily says, her voice mellow and non-emotional. "We know you were there. We know either one or all three of you are responsible for the deaths. We have evidence that puts you at the scene, so you may as well talk to us."

"What evidence?" Her words are barely audible in the small, nondescript interrogation room with the sickly off-white walls that reveal years of abuse.

"Let's just say that we can put you there," Cliff answers. "And we can put your boyfriends there right along with you. It's called forensic science, and you guys didn't do a very good job of covering your tracks. You left behind all kinds of DNA samples, which is irrefutable proof of you being in the house. We've got an air-tight case against you so you, may as well talk to us." He decides not to mention that they won't have DNA results back for ages.

She shrugs.

"You want to play it cool, Gwen?" Cliff says, his eyes narrowing. "Is that it? I am willing to bet that when we go into the next room and talk to your boyfriends, they'll tell us everything we want to know, and they'll say this was all your idea and you were the one that killed those people—your family. They'll put the blame all on you, Gwen, and you'll take the fall."

"He's right," Emily says, keeping her eyes glued on the suspect. She knows eye contact is important when trying to get a read on what a person is thinking. "But you can get the jump on them by telling us everything that happened there."

She remains quiet.

"Aren't you tired of this?" Emily continues, lowering her voice and leaning across the table to get closer to the young woman. "Isn't this a terrible secret to be carrying around? Let's just get this out in the open so you can put it all behind you."

Gwen shrugs.

"Is one of those men your boyfriend?" Emily asks. "Are they both your boyfriend? Do you sleep with both of them?"

"God, no," she quickly answers, her eyes becoming narrow slits and her lips pursing in anger. "I wouldn't be caught dead in bed with Danny."

"That's Danny Rideout?" Cliff asks, looking at the pad where he had already made some notes before entering the room. "He's not your boyfriend?"

"No." She practically spits the word at Cliff. "He's a creep."

"Then what are you doing with him?" Emily asks.

"He's Ricky's friend, not mine."

Thinking maybe the woman is starting to crack, Emily continues in a soft tone, "Ricky is your boyfriend? Ricky Wright?"

"Yes," she answers, glancing back down at the table.

"So how long have you and Ricky been together?" the detective asks.

"Almost three years. He's a great guy."

"Yeah," Cliff almost grunts, scanning his notes. "I can see he's a real peach. Assault. Break and enter. Possession. Trafficking. Carrying a concealed weapon." Scowling at the woman he'd like to shake into reality, he adds, "He's got a record longer than my arm."

"Ricky didn't do nothin'," Gwen says, her contempt for Cliff now clearly evident.

"No," Cliff says. "He's a sweet little angel. Trust me, honey, he's no angel."

"I'm not your honey," she spits at him, her words filled with hate.

"No," Cliff shrugs. "You most certainly are not. But what you are is a spoiled brat. A kid with a chip on her shoulder. A kid who thinks she's entitled to everything she wants but doesn't have to work for it. You're a drug addict, a thief and a murderer."

"I'm not a murderer," she whispers, slouching further in her chair, pulling her shoulders in and turning her gaze to Emily. "I'm not a murderer."

Recognizing he's hit a nerve, Cliff pulls back and lets the detective take over.

"So then," Emily says, her voice low and steady, "why don't you tell us then what happened at your mother's house. You say you are not a murderer. If that's the case, you are going to have to help us understand who did the killing. It's time for you to set the record straight."

The young woman shrugs.

"Are you protecting Ricky?" Emily asks. "Is that it?"

She looks away.

"You have to ask yourself, Gwen," Emily prods, "would he protect you? Or would he turn all the blame back on you if he thought for a second it would make it easier on himself?"

"He loves me," Gwen says.

"Does he?" Emily pauses and studies the suspect. "Does he love you enough to take on all the blame in order to protect you?"

She refuses to answer or look at the detective.

"Think about it, Gwen," Emily continues. "You are going to jail and you are not going to see Ricky for a very long time. You can make this easier on yourself and still have a future, but not if you don't cooperate."

"He wouldn't blame me," Gwen whispers, slowly turning her gaze back to the pretty brunette who she thinks looks more like a model than a police detective. "He loves me."

"I'm not arguing the point," Emily says. "So he loves you. So what? You can't be together and I think he's smart enough to know that. He also knows if he makes it look like someone else—maybe his drug-riddled girlfriend who was pissed off at her family—did all the dirty work, then maybe we'll go easier on him. So you have a choice to make." Emily pauses and then asks, "Do you want some time to think about it?"

There is a long pause. Cliff holds still, almost not breathing.

Then the woman looks up. "Okay." Gwen stares into Emily's eyes. "I will tell you what happened, but I don't want *him* to talk anymore."

Cliff nods. "Okay, Gwen. You win. I won't say another word. I'll just sit here and listen just as long as you tell us everything, but if I think anything I'm hearing is a lie, I will call you on it."

She nods. "Can I have something to drink? Coffee or pop?"

"How about water?" Emily asks.

The woman nods. "Fine."

Rising from his chair, Cliff says, "I'll get it. Give me two minutes to get back and then I want you to tell us everything that happened that night, and I want the truth."

She says nothing but glares at Cliff as he leaves the room.

34: Just the facts

"So." Gwen takes a deep breath and then exhales forcefully, blinking her eyes repeatedly as if she's trying to focus on something.

"No bullshit," Cliff says, his tone firm. "We want the whole story just like it happened, and stick with the facts."

The young woman glares at him, then focuses on the young female detective. "This is how it went down," she begins. Then she has to stop to gulp down a mouthful of water from the bottle, the plastic so thin it crunches under her grip. She sets the bottle on the table and keeps her eyes glued to it.

> We had been watching the house for a couple of days.
>
> It's my fault we ended up here. I had been talking about how rich my mom was since she lived with this wealthy guy back here at home and one day, about a month ago, I jokingly said I wondered what would happen if I showed up at their house and asked them for money. I wondered if they would give it to me.
>
> I was just kidding around, you know? But Danny would never let it go. He kept pressuring Ricky to make me bring them to the house. I didn't want to at first. I kept telling him no because I thought I never wanted to come back here again, but they wouldn't drop it, and before I knew it, we were on our way to Nova Scotia. Deep down inside though, I guess...maybe I really wanted to come back, so it didn't take much arm-twisting.
>
> We drove here from Alberta and we made good time in Ricky's car, the beat-up thing that it is. It took us over three days to get here, but we never stopped for much. We didn't

have much money and we had to save what we had for gas 'cause we knew if we got stranded somewhere along the way there wasn't anybody we could call to come to come and get us. We'd be in big trouble and we'd be stuck.

When we needed to sleep, we'd find a place alongside the road somewhere, pull over and sleep in the car. We ate in the car when we had food that we took when we'd stop at corner stores and gas stations. Sometimes we even went to the bathroom in the car when we didn't want to stop, that's how much in a rush we were to get here. We'd pee in a bottle and then just throw it out the window. ... There's bottles of pee all along the way from Alberta back to Nova Scotia.

She laughs, keeping her eyes glued to the water bottle.

When we first got here, we kept our distance. You know, we'd drive by the house and never slow down. We'd just get a quick look at the big ole place and then keep on going. My mom did real good for herself, I'll say that much.

She pauses and sighs heavily.

After a day of doing that, we started parking on the road that runs along by the trees that border on the backyard. I think it's called Elm Street, or something like that. I'm no good with place names. From there, it was easy to get to the house. Not much security for a rich family.

At first, we'd stay in the trees and watch them from there. Then, at night, we'd sneak up to the house and look around. We did that for a couple of days and we'd be careful no one could see us but I got the feeling mom knew someone was around.

She shrugs.

I don't know why I felt that way but she just started acting funny, and it made me think she could sense someone was hanging around or something. It was kind of weird but my mother was always strange like that. It was like she had a sixth sense. Sometimes it gave me the creeps.

Gwen pauses and takes a long gulp of water. She scratches the back of her neck with her dirty fingernails.

I tried calling her a few times too, you know, just to feel her out about things, but as soon as she answered the phone I lost my nerve and couldn't think of anything to say, so I usually just listened to her to breathing for a few seconds and then I'd hang up. I knew she could hear me breathing over the phone, too, but I just didn't know what to say to her.

At first, it was kind of fun, but then I found it gave me the creeps to see my mom and my little boy out there in the backyard and in the pool. I hadn't seen them in a long time and I was surprised to see Carter had grown so much. He was around three when I left him and I couldn't get over how big he was. He was kind of fat, which surprised me because I'm not fat and his father was never fat, but I guess that's just how he was meant to be.

Anyway, it felt kind of odd to be close to them again and not talk to them, but I knew if they saw me out there our cover would have been blown and we'd have to go away empty-handed. But, deep down inside, I really thought if I went to my mom and asked her for money, she'd be so happy to see me she would just give it to me, but that's not how it worked out.

We didn't see Josh around. I guess he was out of town or something and, looking back, I think it was a mistake that we waited until he got home before we approached them. I think it would have been better for all of us if I had gone to my mom and talked to her without Josh around, but the guys wanted to wait until Josh came home because they thought we could get more money out of him.

She takes another big gulp of water and swallows hard.

When Josh finally came home, we knew it was time to do what we came here for 'cause we were tired of living in the car. We waited all day and evening, just hanging around and watching the house.

For whatever reason, mom wouldn't let the kids outside to play. It's like she was spooked by something 'cause it was a beautiful day, hot and sunny, and I expected to see the kids playing in the pool or at least out in the backyard, but they didn't come out all day. Maybe she knew someone was out there, I don't know. But we stuck it out and waited until it got dark. It was freaking hot in those woods. We waited until all the lights in the house went out and then we waited until we were sure everyone was asleep.

The guys had come up with this great plan that we would break into the house, make mom and the kids our prisoners and force Josh to give us a bunch of money. They didn't think he would fight back. They didn't think he'd do anything to put his family in danger, but I knew Josh. I knew him better than most people and I tried to make them understand he wouldn't be pushed around. He was too pig-headed and felt he was better than anyone else. I didn't like it 'cause I knew he wouldn't just hand them money, but they wouldn't listen to me.

So, we snuck up to the patio and were making our way to the back doors off the kitchen when Ricky knocked over a flower pot and it broke. Danny was pissed at Ricky for being so clumsy—he actually said stupid—but Ricky ain't stupid. But by then it was too late.

I guess Josh couldn't have been sleeping, because the next thing I know he was at the patio doors and coming out to check around. Guess he just had to see what the noise was, and that's when he caught us. And that's when hell broke out.

It was dark, so he couldn't see our faces clearly but he could see us. "Who the hell are you? What the fuck do you want?" he said, when he saw the three of us standing there like three deer caught in the headlights.

We should have just turned and run, but Josh kept yelling at us and the next thing I know, Danny pulls out this pistol and shoots him. I didn't know Danny had a gun. I swear I didn't know.

It looked like the bullet hit Josh somewhere in the stomach or side, and I could tell he was hit. I watched him stumble backward into the kitchen. His arms went through a couple of those door windows and broke the glass, but somehow, he managed to keep his balance.

She pauses, takes a deep breath.

I guess Josh knew he was in trouble because he turned and ran out of the kitchen. He went through the family room, into the hallway and made it all the way to the front door. Danny told Ricky to go after him and bring him back, so by the time Josh made it to the door and got it open just a crack, Ricky grabbed him from behind and slammed the door shut. They struggled right there by the door and Josh put up a good fight, but Ricky pulled out a knife and stabbed Josh in the arm.

From that point, things just kept going from bad to worse. I think that's when Josh realized he was trapped and it wasn't any good to fight so he just gave up. When Ricky was bringing him back into the family room that's when my mother came running down the front stairs. When she saw what was going on, she turned and started to run back upstairs, but Ricky told her to come down or he would hurt Josh some more, maybe even kill him, he said.

I'm not sure if he would have, but my mother did as she was told and followed them back into the family room where me and Danny were.

If you could have seen the look on my mother's face when she saw me, you wouldn't have believed it. Let's just say there wasn't any warm hugs or greetings between us.

Danny got rough with her right away. He grabbed my mother by the arms and forced her to sit in the big chair and Ricky brought Josh back to the sofa and made him sit there. He was bleeding pretty bad by this time and my mother was crying and screaming at us and asking what we wanted. When Danny told them we wanted money, Josh told him to get lost, he wasn't giving us a fucking penny.

Those were his exact words—'not a fucking penny.'

With that, Danny punched him in the face and I could see Josh's head snap back and the blood fly from his mouth.

She sighs heavily and closes her eyes for a moment.

Then Danny hit him a second time with the handle of the gun and I could see the blood running from his nose. He was hurt pretty bad, I could tell.

Danny told me to go upstairs and get the kids and to bring them downstairs. I didn't want to, but Ricky told me to do what Danny said. I had no idea what Danny was planning to do. I was afraid he'd turn on me if I didn't do what he said. I had heard stories and I was always afraid of him, but Ricky liked him for some fucking reason.

Anyway, I did what Danny told me to do. I went upstairs and woke up the kids. I was actually surprised they were still asleep, considering all the noise, but they were both out cold. I brought them back down to the family room. They were terrified. There was all this blood and everyone was crying and screaming.

Carter had no idea who I was so when he saw what was going on he ran right to my mother and crawled up on her lap. She hugged him tightly, pulling his face to her chest to protect him, and I could see she really cared for him. As for the littlest boy, he hung back at first, but I made him go over and sit by his father. He climbed up on the sofa and sat close to Josh, but he had the strangest look about him and you know, despite everything that was going on, I actually don't think the kid was scared. It's the weirdest thing.

Looking back on it now, I realize that didn't seem right, but it didn't hit me right then.

She stops and digs at the skin on her ankle, causing it to bleed. Glancing at Emily, she shrugs and then continues.

Danny stuck the gun right in Josh's face and told him if he didn't give us money, he'd start killing the kids and then my mother one at a time and he'd make Josh watch.

I guess Josh didn't believe he'd do it, because he still refused. I don't know why he just didn't give us whatever money was in the house. We would have taken it and left... or at least I think we would have.

Danny was pissed. He turned the gun on the small boy, I begged him not to shoot the kid but he told me to shut the fuck up, and I did.

Of course, my mother, being the kind of know-it-all she is, had to speak up and make matters worse. "Are these the kind of people you've been hanging around with Gwen? Drug addicts and bullies who pick on little kids. You've done very well for yourself, haven't you? I'm so proud of you. Look at what you've become."

I told her to shut up. I told her she didn't understand, but she just had to keep on talking. I don't know why she was like that. She could never shut up even when her life depended on it.

"I knew you would never amount to anything, Gwen, but I didn't think it would come to this," she said, sitting there on her holier-than-thou throne. Judging me for things she didn't understand. She didn't know me or what I had been through.

"You could have done much better but you were too lazy and always thought you knew everything," she said.

Nothing had changed in all those years I was away. She just had to keep right on attacking me and that's when I remembered why I left home and never came back.

"You've made a great life for yourself, haven't you?" she said.

I told her she had no idea what she was talking about and she should just shut up, but she had to keep pushing. She wanted to know how I had gotten to this point in my life that I would stoop to doing something like this, so I finally told her. I told her why I turned to drugs in the first place and why I ran away from her. I told her why I left Carter with her.

She was shocked when she finally heard the truth, I'll give her that much.

"Mother, maybe if you knew the truth you wouldn't judge me so badly," I said. "It's fine for you to sit here all high and mighty with all your money and thinking you live with such a great man, but do you really know what Josh Goodwin is like?"

I could see she had no idea what I was talking about.

"Do you know why I never told you or anyone who Carter's father is? I did it to protect you."

She was stunned by what I was saying.

I said, "Josh is Carter's father. I never told you because I knew it would destroy you. *He* should have been the one to tell you."

"You're lying," she screamed. "You're a lying bitch who will say anything to get her own way."

"Am I?" I screamed back. "Look at them, mother. Look at their hair. Look at their faces. Can't you see it? Ask him, mother. Make him tell you the truth."

I think she already knew what I was saying was the truth, but she was afraid to hear it.

"I'll ask him," I said. "Go ahead, Josh. Tell her how you got me pregnant while I was still a teenager and how you then left me to be with her. Tell her how you took advantage of me when I was vulnerable after my father died. Tell her how you wanted me to have an abortion so you could keep your secret from her."

He didn't say anything at first but finally he looked at my mother. "Yes," he said, showing no emotion. He would never cry in front of anyone. "It's true, honey, but we weren't seeing each other yet."

"No," mother said. "I don't believe it."

"It's true," I said. "That's why Josh sent me money once in a while and not tell you about it. He felt guilty for what he had done and he thought a few dollars would make up for it. But he never gave me enough to make up for what he did to me."

"You knew?" my mother asked him. "You knew you were the father and you never told me? You kept it from me for all those years? Didn't you think I had a right to know you were the father of my grandson? How could you do that to me?"

"I didn't want to hurt you," he finally cried.

Maybe it was the first time he ever cried in his whole life, but he actually sobbed like a baby, right there in front of his children.

By then, Danny didn't care to hear any more of this family shit, as he called it. He told Josh he had until he counted to ten to give him some money or someone in the room was going to die.

He started counting and waving his arm around the room, moving the gun from Alex, to Carter, to my mother and then back to Alex. I could see Josh was starting to freak out at this point. He was in a lot of pain and bleeding really bad, but he still didn't think Danny would actually do it.

He was wrong.

By the time Danny counted to ten, the gun was pointing at my mother and my son.

"No," I screamed, but it was too late. The gun fired and my son slumped in my mother's arms. Danny shot my son in the back, just below the neck. I could see where the bullet entered his body by the blood that quickly soaked through his T-shirt.

I screamed, and Danny slapped me in the face.

"Shut the fuck up, bitch," he said. He told Ricky to get a handle on his whore—that's what he called me—or he'd make me shut up. Ricky told me to be quiet but I couldn't. I hadn't seen my son in a long time and now I had just watched him die and he didn't know I was his mother. I may have left him, but I still cared for him.

She uses her left hand to wipe away a tear that had trickled down her cheek while keeping her eyes focused on the water bottle.

That's when I realized none of my family was going to survive this. Danny turned to Josh and asked him if he wanted to see someone else die and Josh begged him to stop. He told him he'd have to go into the den to get the money because there was a safe there up over the fireplace, but Danny said no. He wanted the combination and he said I would go and get it. When Josh refused to give him the combination, Danny told my mother to put Carter on the floor, but she was hugging him tightly to her body and sobbing so hard.

"Do it," he screamed and when she finally placed him on the floor, I could see she was covered in my son's blood.

"Now," he told Josh. "Give us the fucking combination or she's next."

"Okay. Okay," Josh said and spouted off some numbers. I can't remember them now.

Danny wanted to make sure it was the actual combination, so he fired a shot at mother. The bullet hit her in the right leg just below the knee and she screamed. It was horrible.

"This better be the right fucking number," he told Josh, "or the next one goes between her eyes."

Then he told me to take the combination and go and try the safe. I did. It took me a few tries because I was pretty nervous, but I finally got it open. There wasn't a whole lot of money in there, about fourteen hundred dollars. There was a couple of envelopes with some papers in them that I didn't take and an old watch which I thought must have been valuable if it was in the safe, so I took that and ran back into the family room.

Danny wasn't happy when he saw the cash and demanded Josh tell him where the big money was. Both Josh and my mother insisted that was all the cash they had in the house. They said they never keep money around the house.

I believed them. I told Danny and Ricky we had to leave. I couldn't believe what we had done for so little money, but I told them we had to get out of there before someone showed up and caught us. They finally agreed, but Danny wasn't done. He said we couldn't leave witnesses who could identify us.

I was freaking out because I knew what he was saying. He told Ricky we had to kill them all to protect our asses. I couldn't stop them and I watched as Ricky went behind Josh and put his knife up to his left ear and slowly pulled the knife across his throat.

It was the worst thing I had ever seen in my whole life... other than my own son dying. I didn't think Ricky would ever do something like that. Josh was struggling to breathe and then he just stopped and slumped over. I will never forget the gurgling noises he made.

And it wasn't over. I couldn't stop him. Danny stood in front of my mother, placed the gun barrel on her forehead and looked her right in her eyes.

"Run," she told Alex, but he stayed on the sofa.

She refused to beg for her life. She stopped crying and stared back at him, defying him. She blinked, he squeezed the trigger, the gun fired, her brains exploded out of the back of her head and she was dead.

She snaps her fingers to emphasize her point.

All the while, the little boy, he remained still. He didn't cry and he didn't say a word, but I knew he was going to be next.

She wipes at her eyes. "I need a break."

"We'll take fifteen minutes," Cliff says.

He gets up so abruptly his chair tumbles over with a thud. "I need some air."

35: Six crows

"So what happened with the little boy?" Emily asks, her voice showing no emotion despite what she had heard before the break.

"You'll think I'm crazy." Gwen pulls her shoulders in as if she's retreating into herself.

"No I won't. I'm not going to judge anything you tell me. Just as long as you stick to the truth, you'll be fine."

"Okay, then." Gwen says. She glances at the officers sitting across the table from her, then glances away.

"This is the point when everything got really weird. I mean, really weird."

"Can you tell us about it or do you want to rest?" Emily asks, recognizing her change in demeanour. "Maybe you need more time."

"No, no," Gwen says. "I want to get it over with. Let's just do it."

So if you're keeping track, that's three people dead in front of the little boy, including his mother and father. You'd kind of think this kid would be freaking out—I know I would be—but he does not even shed a tear. I don't think he even blinked. Here I am freaking out, and that little kid acts like he's as cool as a cucumber. I can't explain it.

"You kill him," Danny says to Ricky, who is still standing over Josh with the bloody knife in his hand. I kept thinking, why don't that kid run? I know I would have been out of there like a freakin' flash, but he didn't move a muscle. I thought he must've been in shock or something.

"I ain't killin' no kid," Ricky says.

"Fine, asshole," Danny says, raising the gun. "I'll do it,

then, you goddamned wimp."

Ricky says, "Do we really have to? He's so young."

"Yes, you fucking moron," Danny says, pointing the gun at the kid. "He's old enough to tell them who we are. He's seen our faces."

'You really think he'll be able to remember us?' Ricky says.

"We can't take any chances. Do you want to go to jail to save this brat's ass?"

Then the patio doors flew open and the lights flickered a couple of times, then they went out. It was pretty freaking dark in there for a few minutes and then they came back on again.

That's when I saw them.

She glances up at Emily and then looks at Cliff, who had remained quiet throughout her confession, just like he said he would.

"That's when you saw who?" Emily asks.

As Gwen continues, her voice becomes raspy and more like a whisper.

The crows. They were all around the room and they were *looking* at us. It was like they knew what we had done...and what Danny was going to do.

There were six of them. They were the biggest fucking crows I've ever seen in my life, and I could tell they were pissed at us.

They had the darkest, beadiest little eyes, like tiny marbles, and they watched us wherever we moved in the room. I ain't never seen crows like that before.

You could feel them watching us. Their eyes were glued to us. They scared the shit out of me.

Then the boy calmly got up off the sofa, where his father had just died beside him. He stood there, still as a freaking goddamned statue and all covered in blood, and looked at the crows. He blinked a few times...and that was it.

She shakes her head as if she's having trouble believing her own words.

Then he walked to a corner and just flopped there. He didn't try to run away or nothing. He just sat there. But he didn't cry.

It just wasn't normal.

"What the fuck?" Danny said. He raised the gun and pointed it right at the boy.

That pissed the crows off even more. They all started making this freaking loud noise, like they were screaming at us, and it was the worst thing I had ever heard in my life. It was so goddamned loud it cut through the air and you could practically feel the vibrations. I had to cover my ears.

"Make them stop," I said to Ricky. "Just make them stop and go away."

I was literally shitting bricks 'cause I had no freaking idea what those black birds wanted, but I had the weirdest feeling they were there to protect the kid. Those goddamned birds knew Danny was gonna shoot him and they came to protect him.

"Let's get the fuck outta here," I said to Ricky.

I'm crying and now he's finally starting to see things my way.

"Come on, Danny," he said. "Leave the boy alone. We got some money and that's what we came for, so let's go."

Me and Ricky started to head for the doors, but Danny, he gotta be a big shit. He always thinks he knows more than everybody else so he wasn't leaving.

"I'm not going until I take care of that kid," he said.

What happened next was like something out of a horror movie. Danny's about to pull the trigger and those birds, those fucking black devils, started flying around the room, calling and squealing. Then one of them flew right at Danny. The fucking thing grabbed his hand and wouldn't let go. It sunk its claws and beak into his skin just before the gun fired. It pulled so hard on Danny's hand that it tore off a big chunk of skin. It was bleeding pretty bad.

We all jumped when the gun went off. I thought Danny had shot the boy, but he missed.

Danny screamed, dropped the gun in pain, and I high-tailed it through the fucking doors. From the patio I called for Ricky to come with me. Ricky didn't argue with me this time and he ran out the door and off the patio into the back-yard.

But Danny wasn't giving up without a fight. Even though those black birds were swooping down at him like they were trying to get at his eyes or something, he had the balls to pick up the gun and fire it again at the kid. I swear to god, even though Danny pointed the gun directly at the kid, the bullet went nowhere near him.

I could see the kid clear as day and as gun went off, he raised his two little hands up in front of his face, palms out, like he was telling someone to stop. I'm telling you, the kid stopped the bullet.

She brings her hands to her face and wipes her eyes. She snuffs back tears before continuing.

I know you think I was on drugs or something, but I swear I wasn't. That's just how it happened. Just like I said.

Danny turned tail and came running out to join me and Ricky in the backyard. "Let's get the fuck out of this place," he said. 'There's something weird about that kid."

He didn't have to tell me twice. When I glanced back I could see the crows were still flying around the room, swooping and gliding. Then they all just settled down all at once.

"Wait," I said to the guys.

We watched as those goddamned crows landed in front of the patio doors. They formed a freaking line across the doorway just like they were telling us not to come back.

They were warning us. Those crows were protecting Alex and that's when I knew.

She stops talking. After a few seconds. Emily says, "That's when you knew what, Gwen?"

"That's when I knew he is the chosen one. He is the golden child."

"What do you mean? Who is the chosen one?"

"Him," she says, her irritation rushing to the surface. "The boy. My grandmother used talk about some members of our family being the 'chosen one' or the 'golden child.'"

"And what does that mean?" Emily asks.

"I don't know for sure, but Nanny used to say the chosen ones had a special connection with the crows and the connection gave them special abilities," Gwen says. "I never believed those stories, but I believe them now after what I saw in the house. That kid is special."

"And this grandmother? This would be Lily's mother?"

"Yes," Gwen nods.

"Is she the same one who gave you the black onyx ring we found on your finger?"

"Yes," the suspect nods again. "Why?"

"I was just curious," Emily says.

"How did you know she gave it to me?" Gwen asks, her eyes narrowing to slivers.

"I want to talk some more about these 'chosen ones.' Tell me more about them."

Gwen shrugs. "All I know is that, according to legend, some people in our family have a special ability to bond with the crows around here and I'm telling you that kid has the power."

"So you think he is this 'golden child,'" Emily says.

"Yes," Gwen insists. "Alex is the chosen one."

36: The phone rings again

Where did the time go?
Cliff Graham looks at the calendar in mild disbelief.
Seems like only yesterday when I started this job. ... So much has happened in all those years.
It's December 23, the last official day of his police career, almost thirty years in the Royal Canadian Mounted Police. He could have hung up his Stetson several years ago and received a full pension, but he just couldn't bring himself to do it. He wasn't ready to leave it all behind.
But now, I'm ready for a change. Today, he thinks, *I won't look back.*
He understands that, when he walks out the door this afternoon, it will be the last time he leaves as an active member of the force. The next time he enters this building it will be as a civilian.
But it's time.
The thought gives him goose bumps. *What will I do with myself?*
He puts the last of his personal items into the brown banker's box. His gaze lingers on the photos of his children when they were just youngsters that had sat on his desk. *How fast the kids have grown up.* It seems like yesterday when he graduated from depot and started his career, when his children were babies. Now, here he is, about to enter the world of retirement and they are out on their own.
A lot has happened in those years, he thinks, but he has no regrets, because he knows he always did the best he could every day he wore this uniform. He's proud of his years of service. Now, though, he's actually looking forward to having the time to do the things he's always wanted to do. He and Julie are working toward

reconciliation after all these years apart, and they are even planning a trip together in the spring to someplace warm and probably expensive. He chuckles.

Wherever she wants to go.

They've been discussing the possibilities since Julie brought it up following Carly's graduation last June, but so much was happening back then they got sidetracked. But lately, they appear to be reconnecting just like they did in the early years, before life happened. He's happy they've reached a place in their lives where they can put their differences aside and look to the future—a future she apparently wants to share with him.

He wasn't sure at first if he wanted to get back together with Julie because, after all, she was the one who broke up with him. She was the one who took the children when they were still young and moved to B.C. But he's adult enough to know he has to let go of that grudge if he wants to have a second chance with her, which is all he's been thinking about lately.

He leans back in the green swivel chair and clamps his fingers behind his head. *Life is finally good and it's time to walk away. It's time to put me first.*

Despite having to deal with some sensational cases during his time in Liverpool, Cliff feels he's leaving the town in pretty good shape...unless, of course, the crows have something different to say about it.

As he leans forward to place the lid on the box, the phone rings. Cliff gives a little jump.

Who could be calling today of all days? Don't they know I'm retiring?

"Cliff Graham here," he says, placing the receiver to his ear, amused by his weak sense of humour. "How can I help you?"

"Is this the soon-to-be-retired Cliff Graham?"

Cliff recognizes the voice of Kate Webster, the hotshot lawyer he's locked horns with on more than one occasion over the years. He's also considered her an ally in the pursuit of justice. Even when they were on opposing sides he always had great respect for her. *And she's a damned good lawyer at that.*

"It's me," he says with a smile. He feels good about talking to her on his last official day at work.

"I'm just calling to extend my congratulations on doing a wonderful job with the detachment over the years and to wish you all the best in your retirement. You've certainly earned it. I know it can't be easy for someone like you to finally let go, but I want you to know you can leave with your head up. A sign you were a good commander is that you've always had the respect and support of your officers and, by and large, of the whole community."

"Well," Cliff pauses. He's never figured out how to handle complements and praise. "Thank you for saying so, Kate. I do appreciate it, but I was really just doing my job."

"I mean it. There were times when you were a tough adversary, but through it all I always had a great deal of respect for you and how you conducted yourself. I always knew where I stood with you and I knew your primary focus was to make sure justice was always served. You never wavered from that, even when things got tough, and that's what made you a good cop."

"Thank you again," he says, feeling himself blush.

"So now what?" Kate asks. "Got any major plans for retirement?"

"I plan to take it easy for a few months and then maybe do some travelling."

"Well, if you need anything, never hesitate to ask. Sam and I are always here for you. We appreciate everything you've done for us over the past few months and you are always welcome in our home. I hope you know that."

"I do," he says. "Kate, if you don't mind me asking, how is the little Goodwin boy doing these days? It has been a few months since everything happened over at the house. Is he okay?"

"He had a rough go of it for a while, but he seems to be adjusting reasonably well," Kate says. "We know there's still more to come, but I think he'll get through it and be okay."

"That's good news," Cliff says. "That was such a tragedy. That's the one thing I won't miss about this job—the senseless violence. I've seen way too much of it."

"Haven't we all," Kate says. "I'll let you go now, Cliff. Enjoy your holidays and I guess we'll see you around."

"I'll see you when I see you," Cliff says. "And thanks for calling."

He glances around the now-bare office as he hangs up the phone. *Wasn't that nice…Guess it's time to go.*

He's about to grab the box from his desk when the phone rings again.

"Hello, Cliff Graham here," he says, wondering if this is a conspiracy organized to keep him trapped here on his last day.

"Hey Corporal," Detective Emily Murphy says from Halifax. "Just a quick call to say goodbye before you fall off the face of the earth."

Cliff chuckles. "I'm not going far."

"That place won't be the same without you around every day."

"I'm sure they'll survive. It's time for this old fart to ride off into the sunset."

"You're not old," she quickly answers.

"Old enough to know when it's time to walk away. But I'd be lying if I said I won't miss it."

"I guess I will be seeing you at the trials in February."

"You will. I can't believe those two pricks are pleading not guilty. What a waste of taxpayer money and the court's time. They should just throw their asses in jail and forget about them. The bastards don't deserve to see another day of freedom as far I'm concerned, after what they did."

"I guess the system says they're entitled to a fair trial," Emily says.

"They didn't give Lily and her family any justice. Where's the justice for that little boy who will grow up without his mother and father? Just doesn't seem fair to me."

"It is what it is," Emily says, "and it's not up to us. Thank God it's an open and shut case. With Gwen's testimony, we'll be able to put them away for a lot of years."

"Ah, you heard she agreed to testify in exchange for a reduced charge and, naturally, a reduced sentence."

"I did. I hear the Crown agreed to manslaughter."

"Yup." Cliff nods even though he knows she can't see him. "She'll testify and the Crown and defence will recommend she get seven years with eligibility for parole after five."

"Doesn't seem like much for what she did, does it?" Emily says. "At least they'll all be off the streets for a few years."

"She's going to have to live with the knowledge that she brought them to her family's home and was, in a way, responsible for the deaths of her own mother and son. She might as well killed them herself."

"Do you think she feels any remorse?"

"I'm not really sure," Cliff says. "She's a hard book to read, but I'm hoping deep down inside there's some sort of redeeming value in her."

"So, listen," she says. "I was really calling to wish you well in your retirement, and I also wanted to thank you again for all the support and guidance you gave me when I was under your command. I learned a lot from you."

"No thanks necessary, detective. Just go out there and catch those bad guys and promise me you will always be careful. Never do anything foolish. Stay focused and stay sharp. If you do that, you'll do great."

"You got it Corporal. Oh, I almost forgot, Merry Christmas."

"Merry Christmas to you as well," he says. "Have a great holiday."

Nice young woman and a great cop, he thinks, hanging up again.

He rises out of the green swivel chair and reaches for the box. *Time to go.*

And the phone rings again.

He grabs the hand set. "Cliff Graham."

"Hey chief," a man says. "Catch you at a bad time?"

"Greg?" Cliff asks. "Greg Paris? Is that really you?"

"The one and only."

"I wasn't expecting to hear from you today."

"What?" Greg says. "My best friend's retiring and I can't call to wish him well? I feel bad enough I didn't make your retirement party."

"I missed having you here, and you can certainly call any time," Cliff says. "But I haven't heard from you in months I thought you died and someone forgot to tell me."

"Easy, Cliff," Greg says with a laugh. "I'm fine."

"Andrea? Lucy?"

"They're fine too."

"Where are you guys?"

"About that Cliff," Greg says. "After the situation in Liverpool last year, I had to step away from everything. I had to put it all behind me."

"Even your best friend?" Cliff asks. "I've been worried sick about you."

"I know and I'm sorry, but I was literally coming unglued. I couldn't focus. I couldn't eat or sleep, or even breathe, so I needed to make a clean break. I'm sorry if I hurt you."

"I forgive you now that I know you're okay."

"We're in B.C.," Greg says. "Terrace, as a matter of fact. Now that you're retiring, you should come and maybe stay awhile."

"Sounds like a good idea. And you know you can always come and visit me," Cliff suggests.

"No," Greg quickly answers. "I don't think so. No offence, friend, but I don't plan on ever setting a foot in that town, not ever again."

"I guess I can understand that."

"Anyhow, we've put it behind us and we're all doing well now," Greg says.

"I was especially worried about Lucy."

"She's okay. We had a tough time at first, but I think she's got it managed now. She's not dwelling on it."

"Couldn't have been easy."

"It wasn't but she's a strong kid. A lot like her mother," Greg says. "So listen, I really was calling to wish you the best in your retirement and I hope we can see each other again real soon. I miss you a lot."

"Agreed," Cliff says. "Miss those talks we used to have."

"Let's do it soon. And I promise I will keep in touch."

"You better, because now that I know where you are, I'm not letting you off the hook."

"Got it. Merry Christmas to you and yours."

Cliff hangs up and stares at the phone, daring it to ring again.

But that was a nice surprise, he thinks. He's relieved Greg seems okay, but Cliff knows he would never tell him anything different, even if he weren't doing okay.

He grabs his heavy coat from the stand behind the door, slips it on and then slides the box under his arm. He'll stop by and get the old chair some other time. *Let the new guy get his own chair.*

He makes his way into the administration area without looking back. It's late and the detachment is deserted now except for the cleaning lady, Doris, who is emptying trashcans.

"Goodbye Doris," Cliff says. "I'll see you around."

"I hear it is your last day constable," she replies, stopping what she's doing.

He smiles. She's always called him constable. "It is."

"But you won't be goin' far."

He looks at her and considers her comment, but decides not to respond. "You have a good evening, Doris, and a wonderful Christmas."

"You too constable," she replies. "Enjoy your time off, if you can."

He almost asks her what she means by that comment, but thinks better of it. He's had too many weird conversations with Doris over the years and he's not in the mood to engage in another right now.

As he heads toward his older model Chevy Silverado in the parking area, the snow begins to fall lightly. Cliff tries to forget this will be the last time he can use this route. As a civilian, he cannot use the back entrance.

He opens the passenger-side door and places the brown box on the front seat. Then he hears a loud, cackling sound. He recognizes it right away.

"No," he whispers. He spins around and stares at the pine trees that tower over the detachment.

"Shit." There's a gathering of crows huddled in the branches. It's dark and the snow is falling heavier now, but he can see the birds clear enough to count them.

"...five, six, seven," he says. "Seven crows."

He sprints around the Chevy, opens the driver's-side door and slides in behind the wheel. He peers at the birds through the wind-shield that's quickly being covered by the snow.

Seven crows. I wonder what the hell that means.

Epilogue

The calendar may say it's Christmas Eve, but it doesn't feel like it to Samantha Henderson-Webster. She's finding it difficult to get into the festive spirit. But she's got two young boys to think about and she's determined to make a good holiday for them.

A lot has happened this year, she thinks as she cleans up the dinner dishes and checks on the dessert. She hears the others laughing and talking in the living room and she's thankful there's a houseful this evening. If it wasn't for the company, she's sure she'd be jumping out of her skin.

Charlie and his wife, Rebecca, come every Christmas Eve to bring presents for Hunter and to spend the evening. This year they brought gifts for Alex, and extra presents as today is his third birthday. Sam and Kate decided not to emphasize the birthday, considering everything that happened six months ago, but it was everyone's objective to make the little boy feel like he's a part of their family.

It was also nice of Cliff Graham and his family to stop by. It's good seeing him so happy, and she's glad to hear he and his estranged wife, Julie, are getting back together.

He deserves to be happy, she thinks.

But the real surprise this evening was having Oliver Lewis show up without notice. He had been away from Liverpool for several years and everyone, including his best friend, Charlie, had lost track of him. However, it appears he's back to stay—at least for a while, he says.

He looks good, she thinks, remembering the last time she saw him before he went away after his health issues. *That was a rough time*, she thinks, and she's glad he seems to be doing well.

Busily preparing the crystal bowls for the dessert she hopes everyone will enjoy, Sam thinks about her friend, Lily, and remembers the Christmases they shared together. She remembers how much Lily loved the holidays and how she fussed over getting just the "right" gifts for everyone on her list.

She'd like this desert, Sam thinks, fighting hard to keep the tears at bay. Lily loved her food and often volunteered to test-drive Sam's new recipes.

In Lily's honour, she's trying this new recipe tonight. Poached apples with hot buttered rum sauce and brown butter pecan ice cream sound so good she just had to make it at least once.

She can't imagine anyone wouldn't like it. The children will have ice cream. They both love butterscotch ripple so they're easy to please.

"Let's see now," she says to no one. "How many bowls do I need?"

"Need any help, honey?" Kate yells from the living room.

"Nope," Sam promptly answers, thinking she actually likes the respite the kitchen gives her from the crowd. "I'm good. I'll be right out."

Standing at the stove, her back to the door, Sam doesn't notice the figure coming up the back steps nor does she see the shadow on the backdoor window. The knock startles her.

"Jesus," she says, dropping the ladle into the sauce. The hot, thick liquid splashes onto the exposed skin of her wrists. She quickly spins around and makes her way to the door, wiping her hands on her apron and wondering why the visitor hadn't used the front door.

Pulling the curtain aside just a crack, she feels her heart skip a beat when she sees a slender woman with fiery red hair staring back at her, a thin white cloud forming around her head as she exhales in the cold.

"Oh my God," Sam whispers, cautiously opening the back door. "Lily?" She swallows hard. "How can this be?"

Sam isn't sure how she should react. She knows her best friend is dead, but yet here she is seemingly standing in front of her.

Finding the strength to speak, she finally stutters, "Can I help you?"

"Are you Samantha Henderson?" the woman asks, her voice soft, almost lilting, oddly familiar.

"I am," Sam says. "Who are you?"

"I am Zoey," the woman says.

Sam is still puzzled so all she does is shrug.

"Sorry," the woman continues. "My name is Zoey Reeves and I know we've never met, but I've heard a lot about you."

"How?"

"From my sister," the red head answers. "Lily Pittmann was my twin sister."

"What?" Sam feels as if she could faint. "What are you saying?"

"She didn't tell you she had a twin sister?" the woman continues. "I'm not surprised. We didn't tell people we were twins."

"I don't understand," Sam stammers.

"Of course you don't. I wouldn't expect you too. Lily was good at keeping secrets."

"Why?"

"Lots of reasons. May I come in for a few minutes? It's pretty cold out here."

"Yes, of course. I'm sorry," Sam says, opening the door wider and backing up to allow Zoey to enter the kitchen. "Forgive my manners. Would you like something warm to drink, or something to eat?."

"I'm fine, but thanks for offering," the woman says. "I know you and Lily were close friends and I'm sorry for showing up here unannounced like this. I'm sure you must have lots of questions."

"You have no idea," Sam says. "What can I do for you?"

"How is my nephew doing?"

"Alex? He's doing okay," Sam says. "Why? Have you come to take him from me? You can't, you know. Lily left him with me. That was her wish and it's all legal."

"I'm not here for him. I was just concerned about how he was doing. I know he went through a lot and that he's where he belongs. Lily was smart to choose you."

"Would you like to see him?"

"Not tonight," Zoey says. "I don't want to ruin your family gathering. Alex doesn't know about me and I'm thinking he'd have a hard time because I look so much like his mother. I want him to have a good Christmas so I'll come back some other time and see him."

"What can I do for you, then?"

"Well Sam, you have something that belongs to me and I would like to have it back, please."

Sam is almost afraid to ask. "What is that?"

"You have my great grandmother's Bible."

"I don't have it."

"Who does?"

"No one," Sam says. "It's still at the Goodwin house, along with everything else they owned. The only things we took were Alex's personal items and his clothes. Everything else has to stay there until the estate is finalized and they tell me that will take a few more months."

"I really need to get my hands on that Bible," Zoey says.

"I've seen it there and I know exactly where it is, but I'm not sure when I can get it for you. What's so important about that book that you need to have it right now?"

"It's the key to everything."

"The key?" Sam stares at the slender woman, still in shock at how much she looks and sounds like Lily. "I don't understand."

"That's a secret yet to be told, but all will be revealed when seven crows come to the murder," Zoey says, as if she was reciting something. "But time's a-wasting. I must see the Bible as quickly as possible."

Acknowledgements

As you can imagine, creating a book is a major undertaking, and while the writing often takes years and is usually done in isolation, there are always numerous people who play key roles in completing the process. It's appropriate, then, to acknowledge a few of those people who helped bring *Six Crows Gold* to you.

Writing a book is only the first step. Finding a publisher is the next major hurdle and it is not always easy. It is important, then, to thank publisher Brenda J. Thompson and my extraordinary editor, Andrew Wetmore. They are the driving force behind Moose House Publications. This has been an incredible journey. Thank you for your support and guidance throughout the process.

Thank you as well to my friend and fellow dreamer, Marci Lin Melvin, for her many years of support, advice and insights. Her never-give-up attitude and creativity played a major role in helping to shape this book. I could not have done it without her. Saying thank you hardly seems like enough, but thank you.

I must also extend my deepest gratitude to graphic artist Denis Cunningham for his amazing cover design. Capturing the essence of an entire book in one image is no easy assignment, but Denis delivered an image so compelling that it is simply stunning. Thank you, Denis!

I've saved my last thank-you for my most important supporters, my family, especially my wife, Nancy. She has been my rock through the many years I've been chasing this dream of becoming a published author. She is always the first one to give an insightful word of advice and a gentle prod when it is needed. To say I could not have done it without her is an understatement. There are not enough words to say how much I appreciate her.

Finally, a huge shout-out to the fans of these books. Thank you for being patient as *Six Crows Gold* made its way through the creative process. It is my hope that you find the story every bit as intriguing and suspenseful as you hoped it would be.

Enjoy the ride, and stay tuned for *Seven Crows a Secret Yet to be Told.*

About the author

Vernon Oickle was born and raised in Liverpool, Nova Scotia, where he continues to reside with his wife, Nancy, and their family.

Growing up in a small town in rural Nova Scotia, Vernon always wanted to pursue a career as a newspaper reporter. After completing high school in 1979, he attended Lethbridge Community College. He graduated in 1982 with an honours diploma in Journalism and returned to Liverpool to work at the local newspaper, *The Advance*. His community newspaper career spanned 33 years.

In addition to his long list of newspaper awards and honours, in 2012 Vernon received the Queen Elizabeth II Diamond Jubilee Medal, recognizing his contributions to his community, province and country, and in April 2015 he received a Distinguished Alumni Award (Community Leader) from Lethbridge College. He was inducted into the Atlantic Journalism Awards Hall of Fame in the spring of 2020.

As a testimony to his outstanding career, in 2014 the South Queens Middle School in Liverpool announced the creation of the Vernon Oickle Writer's Award, to be given annually to a student who excels in the art of writing, either fiction or non-fiction.